TIED TO A BOSS IV

J. L. Rose

Good2Go Publishing

Tied To A Boss IV
Written by J.L.Rose
Cover design: Davida Baldwin
Typesetter: Mychea
ISBN: 9781943686445

Copyright ©2017 Good2Go Publishing
Published 2017 by Good2Go Publishing
7311 W. Glass Lane • Laveen, AZ 85339
www.good2gopublishing.com
https://twitter.com/good2gobooks
G2G@good2gopublishing.com
www.facebook.com/good2gopublishing
www.instagram.com/good2gopublishing

ACKNOWLEDGEMENT

This book would never be if not for my heavenly Father. I thank over and over for this blessing you have given me, my Lord Jesus. And to my mother and father (Ludie A. Rose and John L. Rose Sr.), the two of you are the strength that keeps me moving forward, and I work as I do to finally make you both proud of me. I love you both more than I can ever begin to attempt to find the words to explain. And lastly, to my girls (LeMeka Jones and Victoria "Vicky" Summerset), I think you two—along with my momma—are my biggest fans, and I just want you to know you're my heart. I love you both.

DEDICATION

This book is dedicated to my niece, Victoria "Vicky" Summerset. I love you, baby girl.

PROLOGUE

Two hours later, ten bags a piece, and still checking out more stores, Monica was ready to check out. Dante allowed her to shop, and even bought gifts for Alinna and Natalie. Just as he was paying for a diamond-faced Movado watch, his phone started vibrating in his pocket again.

"You ready to go?" Monica asked, walking up beside Dante as he was pulling out his cell phone.

"You finished?" Dante asked, seeing Natalie's number on the screen.

"I'm ready," Monica told him, waving for Dante to leave the store with her.

"What's up, beautiful?" Dante said, but then he immediately stopped in his tracks when he heard crying and yelling in the background over his phone. "Natalie! Natalie! What's up? What's going on?"

"Dante! Dante! It's Daddy!" Natalie got out before she started crying hysterically.

"Natalie, talk to me!" Dante yelled, already running toward the exit. "Baby, what's going on? Talk to me!"

"Dante, what's going on?" Monica asked, running and trying to keep up with a surprisingly fast Dante.

"I don't know. Natalie was—!"

"Dante, man! It's Dominic. He was set up!"

"Fuck do you mean set up?"

"He was meeting somebody for some business meeting, and once we got there, all we met was a bunch of niggas with guns."

"Shit!" Dante said as he and Monica stopped at her Jaguar. "What about Dominic?"

"Bruh, he got hit twice. It ain't looking good," Tony T explained. "We ain't sure what's going on right now. The doctor's got him."

"Where the fuck y'all at?" Dante asked, completely pissed off.

"We at Phoenix Memorial."

Hanging up the phone, Dante handed Monica the rest of the bags he was holding as she asked, "What's it about?"

"Natalie's father was shot. He's at Phoenix Memorial, and they're not sure if he'll live," Dante explained.

He then pulled out his left-side Glock from its holster and handed it to Monica.

"You gonna need one. Shit about to get real stupid in Phoenix!"

ONE

DANTE FLEW THROUGH THE streets of Phoenix, ignoring the blaring horns from the different cars which he shot past or jumped in front of. He only had one place in mind that he needed to be. He switched the Benz into fourth gear and fishtailed the Mercedes, swinging a right onto the street on which Phoenix Memorial was located, so read the GPS system inside his ride.

He cut off the Lexus that was slowing down in front of the hospital entrance. Dante then swung the Benz around in front of the Lexus and then slammed on his brakes a brief moment later in front of the entrance. This caused his Benz's tires to scream out as the people out in front of the hospital jumped or rushed to get out of the way. Dante jumped out of the Benz and rushed around the front, catching a quick glimpse of Monica jumping out of her new Jaguar behind his car.

Dante rushed over to the elevator, bypassing the front desk and the four-person line that was waiting. He then dug out his cell phone and called Tony T.

"Yeah! What's up?"

"What floor y'all on?" Dante asked, just as the

elevator door slid open.

"Fourth floor. Room 1107!"

Hanging up the phone and then punching the floor button on the elevator, Dante road the elevator while deep in thought and feeling his anger sizzling the more he thought about what Tony T had told him about Dominic being set up and taking two hits, now fighting for his life.

Stepping off the elevator as soon as the door opened on the fourth floor, Dante went in search of room 1107. He then spotted Tony T stepping around the corner in the direction in which he was heading.

"What the fuck happened, Tony T?" Dante asked as soon as he and Tony T met up. Dante never broke stride and continued his search for the room in which the family was gathered.

"Bruh, I don't know!"

"Who was Dominic supposedly meeting with?" Dante interrupted Tony T.

"He said somebody named Roosevelt," Tony T informed Dante, who sent a hard look his way, just as the two of them reached the crowd of security personnel who crowded in front of room 1107.

Dante walked straight toward the room. Security opened a path, with one of the men holding open the door for Dante and Tony T.

"Dante!" Carmen cried out after seeing him enter the hospital room while she stood at her husband's bedside.

She held out her hand to him. Dante walked over to her, taking Carmen's hand and seeing the tears sliding down her face.

"Carmen, I'm sorry!" Dante told his mother-in-law, wrapping his arms around her as she leaned against him. "I swear, I'll deal with this!"

"I know, sweetheart," Carmen softly replied as she lightly patted Dante's chest.

She then looked back to her husband and said, "The doctor says that Dominic was very lucky, Dante! The bullet that entered his chest missed his heart by inches, and they were able to remove it and the other one that went into his leg. He will have to walk with a cane from now on, though."

Shaking his head while staring at his father-in-law, Dante looked away and began searching the room for his wife.

"Where's Natalie, Carmen?"

"She left to go to the ladies' room," she answered while staring down at Dominic in the hospital bed.

Balling up his face at what Carmen had just told him, Dante looked back behind him at Tony T, who stood a few feet away.

"Go check on Natalie."

Nodding his head, Tony T turned to leave, just as Monica entered the hospital room.

"Dante, I just saw your wife leaving."

Spinning around to face Monica, Dante asked, "Which one?"

"Natalie!" she replied. "Why is she moving around without Gomez?"

Taking off past Monica, before she could fully finish what she was telling him about Natalie being without protection, Dante burst out of the hospital room, just as Alinna, James, Kerri, and a team of six security men were rushing up the hall.

"Whoa!" Alinna said, grabbing Dante as he went to rush right past her. "What's going on? Where you going?"

"Natalie's out without protection?" Dante answered.

A second later, he was off, running toward the elevator.

"James, go with him!" Alinna told her friend and personal bodyguard assigned to her by Dante himself.

She then looked up to see Monica rushing past her and following Dante.

* * *

Once back on the ground level, after stepping off the elevator, Dante called Natalie's phone and was sent straight to voicemail.

"Shit!" he said, trying her phone number again as he jogged out the front entrance of the hospital.

Dante hung up the phone after getting her voicemail again. He then looked around for his ride, remembering that he left it right in front of the hospital.

"What the?"

"Dante!"

Looking behind him after hearing his name being called out, he saw both Monica and James rushing out the front door.

Dante then addressed Monica: "Where the fuck is my car?"

"Come on!" Monica said, taking off and leading both Dante and James across the parking lot to where she parked his Benz.

Dante took the keys from Monica and got behind the wheel. Monica rushed around to the passenger side while James climbed into the backseat. Dante then started up the Benz. Within seconds, he was peeling out of the parking space toward the exit.

"James. Call Tony T's phone!" Dante ordered as he was speeding up the street away from the hospital.

"And tell him what?" James asked while doing as he was told.

"Tell him to ask Carmen if she knows where Fredrick Roosevelt lives," Dante inquired, shifting gears and picking up speed.

"Dante!" Monica called out, getting a brief glance from him. "Isn't Fredrick Roosevelt the member of the Council Covenant you told me you had to kick out?"

"Yeah!"

"So, what—!"

"Dante!" James called out, interrupting Monica. "I just got Roosevelt's address from Carmen."

"What is it?" Dante asked, turning the GPS system back on and programming in the address which James called out.

* * *

Natalie immediately left the hospital after finding out who was responsible for her father being shot and laid up while fighting for his life. She drove one of the Range Rovers that was issued to security. After a bit of a drive, she pulled up in front of Fredrick Roosevelt's mansion and was surprised to see the front security gate wide open and no security guards in sight.

Natalie looked over at the front door of the mansion and saw that the door was wide open just like the gate. She reached over and grabbed her purse, digging inside and pulling out the .38 Special that her father had given her for protection. She climbed out from the SUV and shut the driver's side door. She then saw an Expedition that was parked in the corner of the mansion grounds, which she hadn't noticed when she first drove through the gate.

Natalie then walked across the parking grounds to the front door of the house. She slowly entered the mansion, looking around to see that the place was torn up and everything was thrown all around. She then made her way further into the house. She was just about to call out for Roosevelt, when she heard what sounded like a group of people running. She then ducked at the loud sound of a gun going off.

Natalie glanced back and saw the hole in the wall right behind her head, just as more shots were fired. She broke into a run and headed into the sitting room while letting her .38 ring out.

Boom! Boom! Boom!

Natalie ducked behind the sofa. She then peeked out around the side and saw five suit-wearing gunmen. She ducked back behind the sofa and reached overhead and let the .38 ring out once more.

Boom! Boom! Boom!

Hearing the clicking sound, which announced that her gun was empty, Natalie cursed under her breath at her luck.

"Come on out, lady!" Natalie heard one of the men call out to her while she was trying to think what she was going to do next.

In that split second, she noticed the hallway along the stairwell. She immediately took off in the direction of the hallway, when she was snatched up around the waist.

"Aggghh! Let me go!"

* * *

When Dante arrived at Roosevelt's mansion, the front gate was still wide open. As he swung his Benz inside the gate and up the long driveway, he noticed one of his security Range Rovers that was parked beside Roosevelt's Lincoln Continental.

"Dante, look!" Monica exclaimed, pointing toward the Expedition parked alongside the mansion.

Dante peeped the Expedition as he was turning off in front of the mansion. He slammed on the brakes right as he heard screaming and saw five men rushing out of the mansion door.

He was already out of his Benz and pulling out his Glock when Monica cried, "Dante, it's Natalie!"

Boom! Boom! Boom! Boom!

Dante let off shots and immediately saw two men fall and a third one stagger backward and grab at his chest. Dante then swung his banger toward the guy who was holding Natalie around the waist while his right hand gripped her by the throat. He peeped James slide up on his left side while Monica was farther away out on his right.

"Let her go!" Dante growled as he began walking closer to the two remaining men.

"Who the fuck?"

Boom!

"Dante!" Monica yelled as she watched him stagger backward.

He soon regained his balance as both he and James opened fire. Monica then watched the man who was holding Natalie release her, after his face was split open by a bullet sent from either Dante or James.

Monica rushed over to Natalie and wrapped her arms around her. She started to walk her away, but both she and Natalie jumped at the two sudden shots that rang out. She looked over at Dante and saw him standing over the body of the last of the five men to fall.

"Dante!" James called out, walking up beside his friend. "Bruh, we need to get the hell outta here!"

Dante slowly turned away from the body of the guy who had shot him. Dante told James to get the Range Rover as he walked over to the Benz where Monica sat in the backseat along with Natalie.

TWO

ALINNA RECEIVED A CALL from Monica about Dante being shot, losing a lot of blood, and then passing out while he was driving all of them back to the hospital. Alinna met the women, James, and Dante in the front of the hospital, with a medical team.

Alinna almost lost her mind with worry as she waited for Dante to get out of surgery. He was having the bullet removed from his chest. Dante's doctor finally appeared and informed everyone that Dante was out of surgery and would be all right; however, he would need plenty of rest.

"Thank you, Doctor," Alinna replied, sighing in relief. "Can we see him?"

"As soon as he's transferred to a room, I'll have a nurse come and get all of you," the doctor informed Alinna and the others, before reminding them all, "Remember that he needs rest!"

"Knowing Dante, that's not happening!" Monica said under her breath as the doctor left the waiting room.

"What the hell happened?" Alinna angrily asked, turning and facing James, Monica, and Natalie.

"It was my fault!" Natalie said softly as tears fell down her face. "I went out to Fredrick Roosevelt's mansion. But when I got there, the front gate and the door were wide open, and there were five guys inside."

"Where's Roosevelt?" Alinna asked, just as they heard someone scream out Dante's name.

She and the others rushed from the waiting room and out into the hallway to see a team of six nurses surround a bare-chested Dante who was ignoring the team as he continued walking toward his friends.

He was wearing Kenneth Cole pants and square-toed Kenneth Cole shoes while carrying his bloodied button-down shirt gripped in his right fist.

"I told you he wouldn't listen!" Monica said as she and the others rushed after him.

Pushing through the team of nurses with James leading the way, Alinna called out to Dante and grabbed his arm.

"Dante, what the hell are you doing?"

"I wanna talk to Carmen," Dante answered while still walking and heading in the direction of Dominic's room.

"Dante, the doctor said—!"

"Mr. Blackwell!" a member of the hospital security team called out as he rushed around in front of Dante and the others.

He held out his hands to stop them, just as Dante kicked him in the midsection. The guard felt the pain immediately as Dante's shoe slammed into his stomach.

Dante then continued to walk past the hospital security guards, who were now laid out in the middle of the floor, and the same team of nurses that were crowded around him. He ignored the stares from his own security team that was stationed in front of Dominic's hospital room door. He then snatched open the door and stepped inside.

"Oh my God! Dante!" Carmen cried out, after hearing the door open and seeing her bandaged son-in-law. "What are you doing out of bed? You've just been shot, Dante!"

"What's going on, Carmen?" Dante asked, ignoring her concern about his well-being. "Something's going on here that I'm not being told."

"What are you talking about, Dante?" she asked, looking from Dante over to Alinna and the others before she turned and faced Dante again. "What exactly happened back at Roosevelt's place?"

"I think someone kidnapped Roosevelt," Natalie spoke up, drawing everyone's attention to her.

She began explaining how she drove to Roosevelt's mansion to confront him about her father, only to find the front security gates wide open with no security personnel in front of the house. She then told everyone that the front door to the mansion was wide open as well. She continued her story and explained how she walked inside and was then shot at by five men, who were, in turn, all killed by James, Dante, and Monica. She ended with the part about Dante being shot by one of the men who had been shot but was not dead—yet.

"So you didn't see any sign of Roosevelt or his wife, Evelyn?" Carmen asked her daughter, seeing Natalie shaking her head no.

"What's going on, Carmen?" Dante asked his original question again, meeting Carmen's eyes once she looked back to him.

Carmen sighed deeply while slowly shaking her head.

Carmen then looked back at her husband and after a moment said, "I'm not exactly sure what's going on, Dante. I just recently found out about a few incidents. But we've never been able to figure out who was behind them."

"What incidents, Carmen?" Dante asked as the hospital room door swung open and both Tony T and Gomez entered the room.

"Where in God's name have you been?" Carmen angrily asked, directing her question at Gomez. "Why weren't you here to protect my daughter like you're being paid to?"

"I—"

"He did as I told him, mother!" Carmen heard a voice behind her announce.

Natalie continued, "Harmony was having problems, and Tony T couldn't get away while working, so I sent Gomez to pick up Harmony and bring her here so the doctor could have a look at her and the baby."

"That's where I just came from," Tony T added.

"I'll talk with Gomez later," Dante spoke up, once more demanding everyone's attention.

He looked at Carmen and again asked, "What's going on, Carmen? What are these incidents you were talking about?"

After sighing again, Carmen explained, "We've had to change locations for pick-up for shipments twice so far, and we've also had a few clients under the Council Covenant's protection that were attacked and robbed."

"Wait a second!" Dante cut in. "Didn't you tell me that even though the Council Covenant is made up of Dominic, Roosevelt, Atlas, and the other three members who filled the now-empty chairs, doesn't each member still have their clients?"

"That's correct, Dante," Carmen answered, noticing the familiar expression on his face whenever he was putting things together inside his mind.

"What are you thinking, Dante?" Alinna asked, also noticing the look on his face, which she knew well herself.

Dante looked behind him after hearing some commotion coming from the room door. He looked at James and Tony T and nodded for them to both check on what was going on.

He then looked back at Carmen and asked, "Carmen, you keep records of everything dealt with each member of the Council Covenant, right?"

"Of course," she answered. "I keep a copy, and there's also a copy locked in the office safe at the Council building. Why?"

"I wanna look over those papers," Dante told her.

"Yo, Dante!" Tony T called from the door.

"Yeah!" Dante answered, directing his attention back to the room door where Tony T stood halfway inside the room.

"Bruh, it's the doctor out here!" Tony T said. "He's demanding to see you and Dominic."

"Let 'im in," Dante told Tony T.

After a few minutes, Dominic's personal physician entered the hospital room with his face balled up, and stared at Dante.

* * *

Dante allowed the doctor to check his bandages, and then he picked up a prescription for pain medication. He had Tony T leave a team of six men inside Dominic's room to guard over him as he and the others left the hospital. Dante then rode with Carmen while James drove his Benz and took Alinna, Natalie, and Monica back to their house.

"Dante, are you sure you're okay?" Carmen asked him, sounding like a worried mother while looking over his wounded chest.

"I'm all right, Carmen," Dante replied.

Dante allowed Carmen to play mother and check his bandages, even though the doctor had just done so.

"Carmen, tell me something. Did Dominic ever get into it with Roosevelt?"

"I've told you before, Dante," Carmen started as she sat back and stared over at her son-in-law, "Roosevelt didn't get along with any of the members. He was always the outspoken one."

"But had he ever gotten into it with anyone who

would have made you believe that things would get violent?" he asked as he sat watching a now quiet Carmen slowly turn her head and look out of her window.

"Talk to me, Carmen! If you want me to help, you've gotta tell me what's going on!" Dante continued.

Carmen remained quiet and continued to stare out the window. She debated whether or not to admit to Dante what she kept back not only from him but from her daughter as well. She heard him call her name again, so she looked back over at her son-in-law.

Carmen then spoke after a brief moment and said, "Dominic and Samuel Atlas got to the point of violence."

Surprised by what he had just been told, after remembering the openly friendly Samuel Atlas from the first and only meeting with the lasting members of the Council Covenant, Dante asked, "What happened between the two?"

Carmen remained quiet for a minute as she looked away from Dante.

She then turned back toward him and answered, "Samuel and I had an affair when he first joined the Council Covenant. Dominic found out because he had me followed. I almost lost my marriage because of the affair."

Dante now understood the connection between Carmen and Atlas at that meeting. Dante then quickly changed the subject after seeing the embarrassed expression on his mother-in-law's face and asked, "How long has Roosevelt been a member of the Council Covenant?"

"Other than me and Dominic, Roosevelt is the oldest member. He's been a part of the Council Covenant for more than twenty years. Samuel was the last member to join in the last nine years," Carmen explained.

"Nine years, huh?" Dante repeated, just as the limousine pulled to a stop.

"What are you thinking, Dante?" Carmen asked, seeing that look on his face again.

"I'm not sure yet!" Dante answered as he nodded toward the door which the chauffeur had opened.

Once they were out of the limo, Dante walked his mother-in-law up the stairs and into her and Dominic's mansion. James followed behind as Carmen quietly led the way. Carmen disappeared upstairs once they got inside, leaving both Dante and James waiting in the living room downstairs.

Dante nodded to one of the security guards who walked by, and then said, "James, something ain't right, fam!"

"What you mean?"

"It's just this whole thing with Dominic and now Roosevelt being kidnapped, and then I just got this crazy feeling about this dude Samuel Atlas! Shit not adding up, bruh!"

"So, what you think?"

"Dante?" Carmen cried from the top of the stairs, drawing both Dante's and James's attention as she rushed down the stairs and handed a cell phone to Dante.

"It's Roosevelt. He's been calling Dominic's phone back to back," she told him.

Taking the phone and seeing that someone was on the line, Dante placed the phone up to his ear and said, "Roosevelt?"

"About fucking time someone answered!" Roosevelt yelled into the phone. "I need fucking help. Now!"

THREE

Alinna Lay Across The bed in her, Natalie, and Dante's bedroom. She was on a conference call with Harmony, Vanessa, and Amber. She told her sisters about Dante getting shot, and she wasn't surprised when Vanessa went off wanting to know if her brother was okay and where he was.

"Vanessa, calm down, girl!" Alinna told her, looking up as Natalie entered the bedroom. "You know how Dante is. Yeah, his ass got shot and now he out in the streets with James trying to figure out who's responsible for shooting him and Dominic."

"Wait!" Amber spoke up now. "You say Dominic got shot?"

"Ain't that who y'all work for, Alinna?" Vanessa asked.

"First off, we don't work for nobody, Vanessa. And, secondly, Dominic is Natalie's father. He's the one that was supplying us at one point," Alinna explained.

"So, who the hell shot him?" Harmony asked, speaking up.

"That's what—! Hold on, y'all!" Alinna told her girl as Kerri walked into the bedroom. "What's up,

Kerri?"

"Dante just called me, and he wanted me to let you know that he and James found Fredrick Roosevelt. They're on their way here now!"

"Thanks, Kerri!" Alinna told her personal assistant and friend who Dante introduced to her.

She turned back to her phone call after Kerri left, just as Natalie walked out of the bathroom after changing.

"Y'all not gonna believe this!" Alinna told her sisters, motioning Natalie over and then repeating the message that Kerri had just given her.

She then had to explain to Vanessa and Amber who Fredrick Roosevelt was.

Emmy walked into the bedroom while the women were still on the phone, to announce that Dante was home. Alinna told her girls that she would call them back as she hung up and went downstairs.

Alinna stood at the front door and saw Fredrick Roosevelt and a middle-aged, light-skinned pretty woman with him. Alinna then looked at Dante as he entered the front door followed by James.

"Alinna, you know Roosevelt. This is his wife, Evelyn," Dante introduced, before adding, "You may wanna hear what Roosevelt has to tell you. I've heard it already."

"Let's go into the den," Alinna suggested to the couple.

She then stopped and turned around to respond to her husband who had just called her, "Yeah?"

"Where's Natalie?" he asked. "I wanna talk to her."

"I think she's in the office studying," Alinna told her husband as she turned and headed into the den.

Nodding to James for him to sit with her, Dante then walked off to go look for Natalie.

* * *

Natalie looked up from her laptop after hearing the office door open, and saw her husband. She felt her heart pick up speed as he stood staring down at her, wondering what he was about to say to her.

Entering the office and closing the door behind him, Dante leaned back against the door, nodded his head, and then said, "Come here."

Standing to her feet and stepping from behind the desk, Natalie walked over to Dante as the two stared into each other's eyes. She stopped in front of her husband, only for him to use his good arm and wrap it around her waist, pulling her up against him in a hug that she instantly relaxed into, wrapping her arms gently around him, all the while mindful of his wounds.

"Dante, I'm sorry. I wasn't—!"

"Natalie, forget it!" he told her, cutting her off while kissing her forehead. "Just don't ever pull anything like that again."

22

"I promise," she replied, lifting her head from his chest and kissing his lips.

Dante ended the kiss, and then looked at his Kenneth Cole watch and saw that it was 7:45 p.m.

He looked back over at Natalie and said, "I'ma let you get back to your studying. I wanna call Carmen and ask her a few questions. And by the way, Roosevelt and his wife are here. They're in the den talking with Alinna and James."

"Where did you find Roosevelt at?" Natalie asked, releasing Dante and taking a step back.

"Relax, Natalie!" Dante told her, seeing the look on her face. "I know you think he's responsible for Dominic lying in the hospital, but from what he just told me, I wanna talk to Carmen and then your father whenever he wakes up."

"What did he tell you?"

"We'll talk about it later."

"Dante, I want to—!"

"We'll talk about it later, Natalie!" he repeated, cutting her off again in the middle of what she was about to say.

Natalie sucked her teeth, turned angrily away, and stomped around to her desk, dropping back down into her desk chair. She missed the smirk that appeared on Dante's lips before he turned and silently left the office.

* * *

Dante sat down inside his and his wives' bedroom after talking with Natalie. He then sat down at the foot of the wide and overly large bed, pulled out his phone, and called Carmen's cell phone.

He listened to the line ring twice before she answered, "Hello."

"Carmen, it's Dante. You busy?"

"Actually, no. I was just about to lie down. What's the matter? Did you find Roosevelt and Evelyn?"

"They're here at the house," Dante told her. "I wanna ask you a question, Carmen. Who's Edward Randolph?"

"Roosevelt told you about Randolph?"

"He told me to ask you, and only that he was once a member of the Council Covenant."

After softly sighing, Carmen began, "Edward Randolph was a member, yes. But that was before I came into power of the Council Covenant. Randolph was a member while my father was still head, until there was a power struggle between my father and Randolph, which led to Randolph being exiled. That, in turn, led to a war that only ended after the death of Randolph's only son. My father decided to leave Randolph alone, and for years we haven't heard anything—even after my father passed away—until a few years ago. We received a message from Edward offering a deal of partnership to combine the

Council Covenant and the organization he was putting together with three other known drug lords, but both Dominic and me, along with the other members of the Council Covenant, all agreed that we would—! Wait! There was one member among us who felt we would at least meet with Edward Randolph."

"Who?"

"Samuel Atlas!"

"Samuel Atlas, huh?" Dante repeated as his mind began flowing with thoughts and unanswered questions to which he planned on finding answers.

Dante listened to Carmen as she finished telling him the rest of the information she knew on Edward Randolph.

Once she was finished, Dante said, "Look, Carmen, I wanna see everything you have on every member, dead or alive, who's with or was with the Council Covenant. I'll pick up the files on the incidents you also told me about."

"What time will you be here, because I want to go back to the hospital to be with Dominic just in case he wakes up."

"I'll be there early tomorrow morning," he told her, but then said, "I'll also bring you back Dominic's phone."

"Very well," Carmen replied, before asking, "How is Natalie doing?"

"She's fine," he answered. "She's inside the office studying. I'll have her call you."

"Thank you, Dante."

After hanging up with Carmen, Dante sat thinking about everything he had just learned, only for Atlas to return to his thoughts once again. Pulling out Dominic's phone from his pocket, Dante first began looking through his received calls and then his outgoing calls. Most of Dominic's incoming calls were from Roosevelt, Carmen, and even Natalie, but the last four outgoing calls were only to Roosevelt.

Dante then checked the phone book and looked through different names and numbers, only to pause on a familiar name. He slowly smiled and pressed send, calling the number and listening to the line ring three times before someone finally answered.

"Hello."

"Long time no hear. How's it going, Carlos?"

* * *

Alinna looked up and saw Dante enter the den dressed in gray sweat pants, a white wifebeater, and white socks. She noticed that his hair looked slightly wet. She stood up from sitting in the La-Z-Boy that Dante always sat in, to let him sit in his favorite chair. She then sat down in his lap, which he always liked either she or Natalie to do.

"So, have you spoken with Carmen about what we talked about, Blackwell?" Roosevelt asked, speaking up first while staring straight at Dante.

Nodding his head slowly, Dante said, "I spoke with her. I know now who Edward Randolph is, but my question to you is, how do you know it was him who sent men after you and Dominic?"

"Because of what Dominic told me, that's how," Roosevelt answered. "And before you ask, Dominic called me one night and told me to add more men to my security team and not to be surprised if I received a call from Edward Randolph."

"What does that prove?" James spoke up from his position leaning against the wall a few feet away from both Dante and Alinna, with his arms crossed over his chest.

"Who are you?" Roosevelt asked nastily, staring hard at James. "Aren't you the help? Why are you even opening your mouth when business is being discussed?"

"Because! He's my brother!" Dante spoke up loudly, drawing Roosevelt's attention to him again. "And that's a good question. You may want to answer it before I begin to think negatively!"

Roosevelt held the young man's eyes, remembering Dominic's warning about the young killer.

He then sighed deeply and loudly before he began, "Because Dominic told me that Randolph mentioned to him about the new heroin connect the two of us are soon to be dealing with."

"Whoa! What heroin contact?" Alinna asked, surprised at what she had just heard.

"Dominic and I are in contact with a Japanese man named Kevin Kim," Roosevelt told Alinna and Dante. "The two of us were going to bring things to the Council Covenant's attention until we were exiled."

"Does Carmen know about this?" Dante asked him.

"I'm really not sure," Roosevelt answered honestly. "But seeing that she is his wife and the rightful leader of the Council Covenant, I'm willing to believe that he shared this information with her."

"So, how is it that this Edward Randolph guy knows this information, Roosevelt?" Dante asked the drug lord, staring him directly in his eyes.

"*That* you'll have to ask Dominic himself, Blackwell," Roosevelt replied, maintaining eye contact with the young killer.

FOUR

CHECKING THE TIME FOR the fourth time since breakfast, and wondering where in God's name her son-in-law was, Carmen made the decision to just call Dante on her way to the hospital to see Dominic. She grabbed her purse and the thick, brown legal folder with the papers that Dante had requested.

Carmen left her bedroom and walked down the stairs that led to the front door. She saw one of the head servants standing at the door speaking with someone with the door half open.

"Who's at the door, Jennifer?" Carmen called out, drawing the servant's attention.

"It's Mr. Atlas, ma'am," Jennifer replied while opening the door all the way to show her that it was Samuel.

"Samuel, what are you doing here?" Carmen asked as she stepped off the steps in surprise. "Why didn't you call first? I could have already been gone."

"I was already in the neighborhood and decided to stop by," he answered as he entered the house uninvited. "I wanted to speak with you about something."

"I'm on my way out, Samuel!" Carmen told him while gripping tighter the folder she held in her hands.

"This will only take a few minutes," Samuel said, stepping toward her as the front door opened, which drew the attention of both of them.

"Am I interrupting?" Dante asked as he, James, and a third man walked inside the mansion.

"Mr. Black—!"

"Is everything all right, Carmen?" Dante asked, cutting off and ignoring what Samuel Atlas was trying to say to him.

Carmen noticed that both James and the other gentleman, who she knew very well, stood on either side of Atlas.

Carmen then looked back toward Dante and said, "Everything's fine, Dante! Mr. Atlas wanted to speak with me about something."

"Oh really?" Dante replied, turning his head to look at the man. "Well, Mr. Atlas, continue what you were just going to say."

Staring into Dante's eyes but addressing Carmen, Atlas said, "Carmen, we can speak at another time. Call me when you're free."

Dante watched as James and their close friend escorted Atlas out the front door.

Dante then looked back toward Carmen and asked, "You sure you're okay?"

"Yes, Dante!" Carmen answered. "I'm just surprised that Samuel would show up. He's never come here, ever!"

Looking back at the face that she hadn't seen in a while as he walked back inside with James, Carmen smiled and said, "How are you, Carlos?"

"I am fine, Mrs. Saldana," Carlos replied, smiling at his ex-employer.

"Dante, where did you find Carlos?" Carmen asked, still with a smile as she looked at him.

"Dominic still had his number programmed into his phone," Dante answered as he handed Carmen Dominic's phone. "I've also hired back Carlos as head of security, and the first thing I want him to do is get rid of the stupid muthafucka at the front gate who let in Atlas!"

"Not a problem, boss," Carlos replied with a smile as he started toward the front door.

However, he abruptly stopped at the sound of Dante's voice calling his name.

"Yes, sir?"

"The name's Dante!" he told Carlos, who nodded with an understanding smile. "Also, Carmen's going to see Dominic, so she's going to need her limo."

"Not a problem, Dante," Carlos replied as he nodded to a smiling Carmen before leaving out the front door.

Turning back to Carmen and seeing her joyous smile, Dante said, "I take it you're happy with my decision to bring Carlos back?"

"Thank you, Dante," she told him. "I assume Carlos explained why he was let go?"

Nodding his head affirmatively, Dante said nothing else about the subject.

He then nodded toward the file in Carmen's hands and asked, "Are those the papers we spoke about?"

"Yes!" Carmen answered as she handed the folder to Dante. "How did everything go last night with Roosevelt?"

"It went how I expected it would," Dante replied. "Let me ask you something, Carmen. Do you know who Kevin Kim is?"

Seeing the surprised look flash across Carmen's face as she took a step back, Dante said, "I take it you know who that is and that Dominic told you, correct?"

"Yes!" Carmen answered, just as the front door opened and Carlos stepped back inside the house with a team of security crowding the front door.

"Your limo is ready, Mrs. Saldana," Carlos announced.

Nodding to Carlos, but then looking back at Dante, she asked, "Is this what all of this is about, Dante?"

"I believe so. But there's still more to this story that I'm trying to figure out. I'm also trying to figure out how this Edward Randolph guy found out about this new connect that both Dominic and Roosevelt managed to come upon. I'ma figure it out, though!"

"I know you will!" she told Dante as she stepped closer and kissed him on the cheek. "Call me if you need me for anything."

Nodding his head in response, Dante looked at James and nodded for his boy to follow as he walked behind both Carmen and Carlos out the front door.

* * *

Back inside the Benz and following Carmen's limo and her security detail out the front gate of the mansion, Dante sat in the passenger seat while James drove. He pulled out his cell phone and pulled up Monica's number.

"Hold on, Dante!" Monica told him as she answered the phone.

Staring out his window while waiting for Monica

33

to come back on the line, Dante looked at James and said, "Food, bruh?"

"Dante!" Monica returned as James nodded his head in understanding.

"You busy?" Dante asked her.

"Not really," Monica replied. "I did as you told me and went into work earlier than was planned. I'm just meeting a few people and getting a look around. What's up, though?"

"Can you get some information for me?"

"Dante, this is my first—! Wait! I just remembered something. I may just be able to get that information you want. What's up?"

"I need you to find whatever you can on some guy named Edward Randolph and also on a Samuel Atlas."

"You say Edward Randolph and Samuel Atlas?"

"Yeah!"

"Anything else?"

"Not right now!"

"All right. I'ma call you back when I got something."

Dante then called Alinna after hanging up with Monica.

"Yeah, Dante!" Alinna replied.

"Where you at?"

"Handling something. Why, what's up?"

"I need you to get Kerri and get in contact with Goldmen and Sutter. Tell 'em both that I want them here in Phoenix in two days."

"What's going on, Dante?" Alinna asked.

"I'll explain later. Let me make some more calls."

After hanging up with Alinna, Dante then punched in his brother's phone number back in Miami.

"We was just about to call you, fam," Dre said as he answered the phone. "You not going to believe what the fuck Vanessa done come up with, bruh!"

"Dre, later for that!" Dante told him. "I think shit about to get real out here in Phoenix, bruh! I may have to turn up out here, and I'ma need some backup for me, Tony T, and James. You down to play?"

"You already know the answer to that shit, nigga! When you need us?"

"I'm sending the jet out there to pick y'all up. Get word to Rafael, and let the Dread know I said I want him to maintain shit until we return. Let 'im know I'll contact him in a few days about a new shipment and to get the orders from the other families on what they want."

"I got you, fam! When the jet coming?"

"I'm sending it out tonight. I'll have Alinna's assistant, Kerri, call with the information on where to meet the jet."

"We'll see you in a minute!"

Dante hung up on Dre and then looked at James.

"So, you really think things are about to get that out of hand to call Dre and Wesley out here?" James asked.

"I think whoever's behind what's going on out here in Phoenix thinks shit's sweet, so I'ma show the city how we get down on some Miami shit!" Dante told James while pulling out a brand-new box of Black & Milds.

FIVE

DANTE STOOD ALONGSIDE HIS Merce-des-Benz AMG C63 S with James and Tony T, who tore himself away from Harmony's side after finding out the rest of the family was coming to Phoenix. Dante watched the G4 jet as it landed and rolled to a stop in front of them. The hatch lifted, and a moment later the steps were lowered. Dre was the first to appear in the doorway.

"There go my muthafuckin' brothers!" Dre yelled as he rushed down the steps.

Smiling at the sight of his brother, Dante started toward Dre, with both Tony T and James smiling and following beside him.

Dre hugged Dante tightly, throwing his arms around Dante in a brotherly embrace. He then released him and looked him over in his black silk Armani suit with matching black button-down.

"I see you living good, even out here, fam!"

"What was you expecting?" Dante replied with a smile as Dre hugged Tony T and then James.

He then swung his head back toward the jet upon hearing, "Andre! Nigga! You better get yo' ass on this jet and get these fucking bags, nigga!"

"Shit!" Dre said, causing Dante and the others to start laughing as he headed back to the plane.

"Daddy!" Dante heard, seeing his daughter, Mya, rushing down the steps and running across the airstrip.

He started toward his daughter as she jumped into his arms. Catching and hugging his baby girl, Dante held Mya in a tight embrace a few moments as she hugged his neck tightly. He then realized just how much he missed her. He kissed the top of her head and held her back a little, smiling as she smiled back at him.

"Look at you, baby girl! You just keep getting bigger every time I see you!"

"I miss you, Daddy!" Mya cried happily, hugging her father's neck again before kissing his cheek.

"I know I better get one of those hugs too," both Dante and Mya heard from behind them as Vanessa and Amber stepped off the plane with their twins, Keisha and Maxine.

Dante then noticed a brown-skinned female who stared straight at him and smiled.

Dante shifted Mya over to his good arm as Vanessa hugged him tightly around the neck.

He kissed her cheek, only for Vanessa to pull back with a balled-up face and ask, "Oh, I can't get no hug, Dante?"

"I got shot, Vanessa. I only use my left arm if I really have to, baby sis!"

Sucking her teeth, she replied, "I forgot about you getting shot. Alinna told us you was out here showing out, but I got a surprise for you."

"What's that?" Dante asked, shifting his eyes toward the jet.

He watched as Dre and Wesley stepped off the plane, followed by his son, Dante Jr., and Dre's son, Andre Jr. They were all then followed by a crew of men carrying the family's suitcases and bags.

"Dante, this is Melody!" Dante heard, shifting his eyes back toward Vanessa, only to see the brown-skinned female he first noticed.

He nodded his head at the smiling woman, but became a little confused by the tears he saw begin to fall from her eyes.

"What's up with the tears?" Dante asked, looking to Vanessa for answers.

Mya then reached out to the crying woman and asked, "Auntie Melody, why you crying?"

Dante released his daughter to the women as the other members of the family walked up.

He then looked at Vanessa as she said, "Dante, her name is Melody Blackwell. She's your birth sister!"

"What?" Dante replied, looking back at the female while meeting her eyes that were the same color as his.

He heard his phone begin to ring and unknowingly dug it from his pocket and answered, "Yeah!"

"Dante! Dante! Where the fuck are you?"

Snapping out of his daze after recognizing Alinna's voice, Dante's face instantly balled up. "Alinna, what's up? What's wrong?"

"Dante, we're being shot at and chased! Where are you? We need help!"

Dante was already rushing toward the Benz while ignoring Vanessa, who was yelling his name. He then lowered the phone from his ear and yelled to Tony T to give the girls a set of keys to one of the two Denalis. Dante then yelled to Dre and the other guys to grab the other Denali as he climbed inside his Benz.

* * *

Alinna yelled over the engine and the sound of gunfire while telling Dante where she and Kerri were. She was trying her best to lose the two black BMWs that were chasing them. She then swung her S-Class Benz Coupe down another street and floored the engine, pulling away a short while, only to look in the rear-view mirror and see the cars catching up to her again.

"Alinna, talk to me!" Dante yelled into the phone. "Where exactly are you?"

"I just turned down—! Shit!" she yelled, ducking after the back windshield was shot out.

"Dante, you're not here yet? You gotta get here!"

"Baby, I'm trying, but you gotta tell me where you're at exactly. Alinna, I can't help if I can't find you!"

Alinna looked around and then told Dante where she was and everything that she was passing. She drove while listening to Dante's instructions, but then she hung up the phone and dropped it into her lap so she could use both her hands to steer the Benz.

"What did Dante say?" Kerri asked from the floor of the passenger seat.

Kerri simply tried to hang on as Alinna surprisingly handled the Benz which she was just recently gifted by Dante.

"We're supposed to meet him on Arizona Avenue. He said he'll meet us there," Alinna answered.

Alinna yanked the Benz down another street and flew past cars alongside her while still staring in the rear-view mirror to see that the two BMWs were still following them.

After a few minutes, Alinna fishtailed the Benz down Arizona Avenue and almost had to slam on the brakes when she saw a crowd standing in the middle of the road. But she quickly recognized Dante standing dead center in the group. She swung the wheel hard to the right, just as all hell opened up.

Alinna hit the brakes, which caused the Benz to slide to a stop before slamming into the side of a building. Alinna then looked back to see Dante and what looked like twenty or thirty other guys open up, shooting at the two BMWs, which both soon lost control. The one car slammed into a light pole, while the second simply slowed to a stop in the middle of the road, with more than one hundred bullet holes.

"Alinna!" Dante yelled, just as he snatched open the driver's door to see that his wife was okay.

He grabbed her from the car and into his arms.

"Dante! Kerri!" Alinna cried, pulling away from him and rushing around the car to help Kerri from the Benz.

"You okay?"

Kerri nodded her yes as she looked up at Dante, only to see the deadly Category 5 storm that appeared in his eyes.

* * *

Dante returned to the mini mansion and was met by Natalie, Vanessa, and the rest of the family and crew members who didn't go to help out Alinna and Kerri. He climbed from the Benz and looked over the roof of the car, just as Vanessa led the rest of the women over to the passenger side where Alinna stepped out and was instantly surrounded.

"Dante!"

Dante heard his name being called and looked behind himself. He saw the woman who was introduced as his sister slowly approach him. Dante slowly looked her over and instantly noticed how extremely gorgeous she was.

"Are you okay?" Melody asked, stopping in front of her big brother.

Nodding his head in response to the question, Dante then asked, "How do I know you're really my sister? Where do you come from? How the hell did you even find me?"

Melody cracked a small smile and said, "Can we go inside and talk? I'll explain everything and answer whatever questions you have that I can answer."

Dante looked down and saw that Melody had put out her hand toward him. He looked back up to meet her eyes and slowly took her hand, which earned an even bigger smile.

Alinna watched as the woman led Dante past her and inside the house. Alinna then looked toward Natalie and heard her say, "Relax, Alinna. That's Dante's younger sister."

"His sister?" Alinna shouted as she looked over at Vanessa.

"She's from Syracuse, New York."

"And how the hell y'all know this?" Alinna questioned.

"A, relax!" Amber spoke up, cutting her off.

"She's his sister. She's proven it to us. We've even spoken with his birth mother, and she got this picture of Dante when he was a baby."

"How was she able to find him way out in Phoenix?" Alinna asked, still not convinced.

"Alinna, come on!" Vanessa spoke up again. "Do you remember who your husband is? I think any and everybody knows who Dante Blackwell is after he turned himself in, only to suddenly walk out of jail scot-free! You better watch the world news! They're still talking about your husband!"

"I wanna talk to this girl!" Alinna said, shaking her head at what she was hearing, with a tight feeling in her gut.

"Why don't you let Dante talk to his sister first,

and then I'm sure Melody will want to talk to her sister-in-law!" Vanessa told Alinna as they all started inside the house.

* * *

Dante listened to Melody as the two of them walked side by side along the bike trail while Mya, Dante Jr., and Andrew Jr. walked together ahead of them. Dante then shifted his attention over to Melody as she began pulling out pictures of the woman she told him was his mother. He instantly recognized his father in the pictures with the woman.

"That's Dad with Mom," Melody told Dante, first looking at the picture and then over toward Dante.

"I know," Dante replied as he stared at the picture unaware that he had stopped walking.

He then shifted his eyes over to the woman in the picture and said, "So, this is what my mother looks like, huh?"

"Mom admitted that she left while you were still a young baby and she was pregnant with me," Melody told him. "She wants to meet you, Dante."

"Meet me, huh?" he asked, looking back at Melody. "Where is she anyway?"

"We live in Syracuse, New York."

"Why didn't she come with you?"

"Because Dwayne just got into an accident right when we found out about you getting locked up on the news! You're pretty famous, big brother!"

Dante looked back at Melody and saw her smile at him, and he noticed her dimples.

Dante handed the picture back, only for Melody to gently push his hand away and say, "You keep it. It's for you."

Nodding his head in thanks, he then said, "Are you staying?"

Nodding her head yes, Melody replied, "Vanessa explained to me that you're in the middle of dealing with something. So, I'll stay until you finish, if you allow me to stay."

"Of course!"

"Will you come to Syracuse once stuff here is in order?"

"Daddy! Daddy!"

Dante looked up just as Mya came rushing over to him, followed by both Dante Jr. and Andre Jr. Dante smiled as he bent down and scooped up his little girl into his arms, ignoring the pain that shot through the left side of his chest.

"What's up, baby girl?"

"Daddy, can we get pizza?" Mya asked, smiling into Dante's face.

"Pizza, huh?" Dante repeated, smiling and looking down at his son and nephew. "What's up fellas? Y'all want pizza too?"

"And a movie!" Dante Jr. added with a big grin.

Laughing at his son, Dante said, "All right, lil' man! I got you! Let's get back to the house, and I'll have Emmy and Rose get y'all some pizza, and we'll watch a movie up in the movie room we have already here."

"Daddy, can Auntie Melody come watch the movie, too?" Mya asked, reaching for Melody, who smiled while taking her niece from Dante.

"What's up, Melody? You wanna hang with us?"

"Of course!" Melody answered, kissing Mya's cheek and then wrapping her left arm around Dante's waist and leaning into him.

* * *

"What's up, gorgeous?" Dante said.

Alinna instantly heard her husband's voice and looked over her shoulder. He was standing a few feet behind her, but she didn't hear him walk in. She turned back to what she was doing inside the closet.

"So, what did she have to say?" Alinna asked over her shoulder.

"I'm assuming you're talking about Melody?" Dante said as Alinna walked past him wearing a peach-colored thong and matching bra while holding an outfit she took from the closet.

"Who else would I be talking about, Dante?" she asked, shooting him a look over her shoulder.

"You wanna tell me what's up with this attitude, when I'm the one that should be heated after I've told you over and over about going anywhere without security?"

"Who do you think you're talking to, nigga?" Alinna asked, spinning angrily around to face him. "Last time I checked, I'm a grown-ass woman. I don't need your permission to do a damn thing!"

"Yeah! You right!" Dante replied with light laughter.

Just as he was turning to leave the bedroom, Natalie walked into the bedroom and bumped into him.

"Hey, baby. What's wrong, Dante?" Natalie asked, instantly noticing Dante's facial expression.

"I'm good, beautiful," Dante told her, kissing her on the lips before stepping around her and walking out of the bedroom.

"What's wrong with him?" Natalie asked, looking back at Alinna after he walked out.

Sucking her teeth, Alinna said, "Dante is just being Dante, Natalie!"

SIX

ALINNA FOUND DANTE, MELODY, and
the kids inside the home theater, after Rose let her
know that Dante was spending time with them.
Alinna caught the way he looked at her once she
entered the theater. She sighed deeply, aware that he
was still mad at her from earlier.

Alinna walked over to the sofa beside where
Dante was seated with Melody, who sat next to him
with her arm wrapped around his middle. Alinna
looked over at Melody as the woman looked up at
her.

"Hi, Alinna," Melody said, smiling up at her
brother's wife.

"Hey!" Alinna replied, emotionless, but then
directed her attention to Dante. "Dante, I need to talk
to you."

"Talk!" Dante replied without taking his eyes
from the screen.

"Dante!"

"What, Alinna?"

"Dante, Alinna's talking to you!" Melody spoke
up, seeing the way her brother was being
disrespectful to his wife. "You need to go and speak
with her if she says she needs to talk with you."

Dante remained where he was sitting until Melody said his name again. He looked at her and saw the look she was giving him. He then shook his head as he stood up from the sofa and started toward the door, with Alinna following behind.

"What's up, Alinna?" Dante asked once the two of them were out in the hallway.

"Dante, Carmen called," Alinna informed him.

She followed alongside Dante as he pulled out his Blacks headed to the back patio.

"Carmen says that Dominic is awake and wants to see you."

"When did he wake up?" Dante asked.

"A few minutes ago," Alinna told him as they stepped outside. "Are you going to see him?"

"Yeah!"

"All right! I want to go too!"

"Whatever! It's your decision."

Alinna sighed at his sarcasm and then said, "Dante. Look, I'm sorry about earlier, okay? I was upset and took my anger out on you. Then I hear this girl is supposed to be your baby sister who just pops up out of nowhere claiming you're her brother. How do we know she's telling the truth?"

"Here!" Dante said while handing Alinna the picture from his pocket that his sister gave him.

Alinna took the picture from Dante. She stared at the picture and then locked her eyes on the older man who was a twin of her husband.

"Dante, is this your father?"

"Yeah!" he answered. "And my mother!"

Alinna stared at the picture a moment, looked back at Dante, and said, "So, Melody is your sister, huh?"

"That's what it looks like," he answered. "After everything's handled here, I wanna take a trip out to meet my mother."

"Of course, baby," Alinna replied, just as a cell phone began to ring.

"That's me!" Dante told Alinna, pulling out his cell phone and seeing that Monica called him. "What's up, Monica?"

"Dante, where are you?"

"At the house. Why?"

"I've got that information you asked me to look for, but I also have somebody I want you to meet. We'll be at the house in twenty minutes."

"Nah, meet me at the hospital," Dante told her. "Dominic woke up and wants to see me!"

"All right! We'll be there in twenty minutes."

"What did Monica want?" Alinna asked as soon as Dante hung up.

"Remember that information I told you I wanted Monica to look up for me? Well, we about to get a better look at who we're dealing with."

"You want me to send for Roosevelt?"

"Have security bring 'im out to the hospital."

Alinna pulled out her phone to make a call to her security escort. She then followed Dante back into the house to get ready to head back out to Phoenix Memorial.

* * *

Carmen hung up the phone with her son-in-law and laid the cell phone back on the bedside table beside her husband's bed as he spoke with the doctor. Carmen waited until the doctor finished speaking with her husband and left the room.

"Dominic, Dante is on his way here now," Carmen said.

"Where the hell is he?"

"Alinna says that they are down the street, Dominic! You need to come down!"

"What the hell has he been doing while I was out of it?" Dominic asked angrily. "Has he gone after Randolph yet?"

"I'm not sure what Dante's plans are, Dominic. But I'm sure that he's putting something together."

"What about Roosevelt?" Dominic asked.

"What's happened to him?"

"Dante has—!"

"Mrs. Saldana!" both Carmen and Dominic heard.

Carmen looked back over to the room door to see Carlos with his head halfway inside the door.

"Yes, Carlos," Carmen replied.

"Dante has just stepped off of the elevator, ma'am!" Carlos told her.

Carlos then stepped inside the room, holding open the door as Dante, Alinna, Roosevelt, and Evelyn all walked into the room.

"About time you decided to show up!" Dominic said angrily once he saw Dante.

Smirking at his father-in-law, Dante kissed Carmen's cheek and then stopped beside Dominic's hospital bed and said, "It's good to see a bullet hasn't changed your attitude. How are you feeling?"

"How do you think I'm feeling?" Dominic asked sarcastically. "What have you been doing while I've been out of commission these few days?"

"Dante!"

Dante looked back toward the door when he heard Carlos call his name.

"You have someone out here by the name of Monica Martin," Carlos said.

"Let her in!" Dante replied, watching as Carlos opened the door and allowed Monica and a light-skinned man into the room. "Who is he?"

"This is who I wanted you to meet," Monica told Dante. "Dante, meet Nash Johnson. Nash, meet Dante Blackwell."

"The living legend himself," Nash said, holding out his hand to Dante for a handshake.

Ignoring the guy's hand, Dante stared at him and then addressed Monica, "Why is DEA here, Monica?"

"What the—? How did—?"

"Dante, it's fine!" Monica told him, handing Dante the cream-colored folder she was holding. "Nash is the one who looked into Edward Randolph and Samuel Atlas for me."

"Dante!" Carmen cried. "Why are you having Mr. Atlas looked up?"

"If I may speak, ma'am," Nash said as he continued before anyone spoke up. "I'm not sure who this Samuel Atlas is that you all keep mentioning, but either this guy is a ghost or you all are mistaking this guy's name."

"What are you talking about?" Carmen asked, staring hard at the young man.

"What Nash is saying," Monica started, shooting him a look, before looking toward Dante, "is there's no one on file by the name of Samuel Atlas."

"But there is a Samuel Randolph who just happens to be Edward Randolph's younger brother," Dante spoke up, reading from the file he was holding.

"Wait a minute!" Carmen said angrily. "Are you telling me that Samuel Atlas is Samuel Randolph, who just happens to be Edward Randolph's brother?"

"Ma'am, it's either that, or this Samuel Atlas you're speaking about is lying and hiding something."

Dante looked over at Alinna as she pulled out her ringing cell phone and walked across the room to answer it.

Dante then looked back at Carmen and asked, "Carmen, where is Samuel now?"

"Last we spoke, he said that he was going out of town on a business trip," Carmen informed Dante, who was still upset at what she had just learned.

"When is he supposed to return?" Roosevelt finally spoke up.

"I'm not sure!" Carmen answered. "He didn't say."

"Dante!" Alinna said, walking up beside him. "That was Mr. Goldmen. He and Mr. Sutter are at the Hilton on 137th and Arizona Drive."

"Who the hell are Goldmen and Sutter?" Dominic asked, staring straight at Dante.

"You ready to talk about Kevin Kim?" Dante asked, ignoring Dominic's question.

He then noticed the surprised look that came across Dominic's face before the Dominican drug lord's face balled up in anger when he looked at Roosevelt.

"You told him?" Dominic angrily asked Roosevelt. "You wasn't supposed to say anything to no damn one!"

"So, how is it that Edward Randolph knows about Kevin Kim, Dominic?" Dante asked him. "He called you with an offer of combining the Council Covenant and whatever type of organization homeboy got put together?"

"I never told Randolph anything and would never agree to anything with that fool of a man!" Dominic answered.

"So, how is it he knows?" Alinna asked.

"Excuse me," Carmen stated as she headed toward the door.

* * *

Carmen dismissed the security that Carlos sent to follow behind her. She then walked to the ladies' restroom and stood at the sink. She set down the cell phone that she picked up from beside Dominic's bed before leaving the hospital room.

Carmen silently stared into the mirror a moment praying that what she was thinking wasn't true. Carmen picked up the phone and called Samuel's personal phone number, which she knew from memory.

"Hello!" Samuel answered on the third ring.

"Samuel, it's Carmen. We need to talk."

"Where are you?"

"I'm at the hospital seeing Dominic, but I'm inside the restroom at the moment."

"Can you get away?"

"Not right now. I need to ask you something, Samuel."

"What's wrong, Carmen? You sound funny."

"Samuel, I need to know the truth!" she told him. "What is your relationship with Edward Randolph?"

Quiet for a brief moment, Samuel finally said, "Carmen, why are you asking me a question like that? Where is this coming from?"

"Samuel, what is your real name?" Carmen asked, just as the phone was snatched from her hand.

Carmen instantly spun around to find herself staring straight at Dante.

Dante placed the phone up to his ear, only to hear Samuel Atlas/Randolph calling Carmen's name.

He held Carmen's eyes and then spoke into the phone, "Carmen's right here, but you're now speaking with Dante."

Hearing silence over the phone, Dante continued, "I know who you are, Samuel. You and your brother, Edward, will be seeing me soon, and whoever else is with the two of you. Let your brother know that he missed Dominic. As for you, I will kill you myself for my wife. You missed her too!"

Dante hung up on Samuel and turned back to face Carmen, who simply stood just staring at him.

Dante then asked, "So, you were still messing with Samuel after all, huh?"

"Dante, it's not what you think!"

"You told Samuel about Kevin Kim, didn't you?" Dante asked, cutting off Carmen as she began to explain.

"I only mentioned it to him, Dante! He really doesn't know anything!"

Dante handed back the phone and then turned to leave the restroom, only to pause at hearing Carmen ask, "What are you going to do, Dante?"

"Kill Samuel Randolph and everybody else who's associated with him and Edward Randolph."

Still standing where she was, even after Dante left the restroom, Carmen felt the tears that began sliding down her face as she thought of how much of a fool she was for trusting Samuel Atlas/Randolph.

* * *

"What's up, bruh?" Dre asked Dante as soon as he stepped out of the lady's restroom, after following his mother-in-law inside.

"It's a work call, bruh!" Dante answered as he and Dre headed back to Dominic's hospital room.

"That's what the fuck I'm talking about!" Dre replied, hyped up at the mention of putting in work after just arriving in Phoenix.

Dante arrived back in the hospital, but he left Dre out in the hallway to let Tony T, Wesley, James, and Carlos in on the plans so far.

Dante interrupted the conversation that was going on inside the room among Alinna, Dominic, and Roosevelt: "I need to know where Samuel Randolph lives!"

"Dante, what's going on?" Alinna asked as she and Monica moved over and stood on each side of him.

"I'ma kill Samuel Randolph!" Dante replied.

He then stared at Dominic and asked, "What's his location, Dominic?"

"Instead of killing him, why not hold him so that we can question him and find out what's going on and who all are involved," Roosevelt suggested, which got Dante's attention.

Slowly nodding his head in agreement, Dante then said, "What's the location?"

After getting the address and directions to Samuel Randolph's mansion, Dante turned to leave the hospital room, only to stop at hearing his name.

He looked over and asked, "What is it, Johnson?"

"If you're going to go out and play, you're gonna need some new toys. Come with me," Johnson told Dante, smiling as he started toward the door.

* * *

"Take a look at this!" Johnson told Dante, once the two of them and Dante's people were outside standing in the hospital parking lot at the back end of his Lincoln Navigator.

He stepped back out of the way and motioned Dante forward.

Dante stepped up to the back of the SUV and looked inside, where he saw two black duffel bags, one large and one extra large.

Dante looked back at Johnson, only for him to smile and say, "Open them!"

"It's fine, Dante," Monica spoke up, seeing the look of concern on Dante's face. "Remember I told you that I had something for you? That's it!"

Dante turned back around and reached for the smaller of the two duffel bags. He slowly smiled upon seeing that the bag was filled with different types of automatic handguns.

Dante picked up a black and chrome Colt .45 from inside the bag. He heard somebody whistle in approval, and he wasn't surprised when Dre stepped up beside him to take the banger out of his hand.

"This is what the fuck I'm talking about!" Dre said with a smile as he looked over the piece, only to shift his eyes back toward his brother as he opened the larger duffel bag.

He handed off the Colt .45 to someone else and took the semiautomatic piece from Dante's hands.

"This a bad muthafucka right here. What the fuck is it?"

"It's an M14 battle rifle with a grenade launcher," Johnson spoke up, smiling at Dre.

"This is some military shit right here!" Dre said with a huge smile on his face.

"Blood clot!" Wesley said, pushing to the front of the group to stand beside Dante. "Fuck the blood clot. Shit! Dis boy say an M14! Me want only the AK. You have one of dem, rude boy?"

Johnson walked to the back of his SUV and dug inside another duffel bag.

A few moments later, he pulled out the piece the Jamaican was asking about and said, "Is this what you're looking for?"

"Blood clot!" Wesley cried, smiling as he took the AK-47 from the man Dante called Johnson.

Looking from Monica and back toward a smiling Johnson, Dante then said, "You work for me now!"

"Hell yeah, I do!" Johnson replied with a smile.

Johnson remembered something that Monica had told him, so he held up a finger for Dante to hold on as he walked around to the front passenger side door. He soon returned, stood next to Dante, and handed Dante something that put a smile on his face.

"Monica told me about you getting shot, and since I now work for you, and seeing how you pay your employees, I feel it's my responsibility to keep you safe now!"

Dante took the metallic black bulletproof vest that Johnson handed him.

He then looked at Monica and saw the small smile on her lips and said, "So you're starting to really give a fuck about me now!"

"Shut up, Blackwell!" Monica playfully told him as she shoved him away. "You still got a promise to keep!"

"Yeah, I remember," Dante replied, thinking about Angela for the first time in a few days.

* * *

"Where is Dante?" Carmen asked, after returning to her husband's hospital room and only seeing Alinna, Roosevelt, Evelyn, and her husband.

"Dante left to pick up Samuel Randolph," Alinna replied, noticing the distraught expression on Carmen's face. She then continued, "Carmen, there will be a meeting here in another hour with you, me, Dominic, Roosevelt, and two other business associates."

"Who are these business associates?" Carmen asked as she walked back over to stand by her husband's bed.

"They're Mr. Sutter and Mr. Goldmen," Alinna answered, just as she heard her cell phone begin to ring. "Excuse me!" she told the group while walking off to the far side of the room to answer the phone.

"Where did you go?" Dominic asked, drawing Carmen's attention around to him.

"I went to the restroom," she replied, but then quickly asked, "How are you feeling?"

"I feel like I'm past ready to get out of the bed!" Dominic answered, just as Alinna rejoined the group.

"So, Alinna," Roosevelt began, getting her attention, "who exactly are these men we're supposedly having a meeting with?"

"I'll let Dante explain that since Mr. Sutter and Mr. Goldmen deal directly with him."

"You mentioned that both Dominic and Roosevelt will be involved in this meeting," Carmen spoke up, focusing her eyes on Alinna. "Have Dante and yourself decided to allow them back into the Council Covenant?"

"Both Dante and I have had a discussion, and, yes, we have decided that both Dominic and Roosevelt will return," Alinna explained.

"When exactly was I supposed to be informed of this decision or even the discussion, Mrs. Blackwell?" Carmen asked with a little attitude.

Alinna slowly smiled while catching yet ignoring the attitude from Dante's mother-in-law, and simply replied, "I'll let any of you who has a problem with the decision that was made discuss it with my husband once he returns."

Alinna's phone rang again in her hand. A big smile appeared on her face when the name showed up on her phone.

"We were just talking about you, Dante. What's up?"

"We're at Samuel's mansion, and homeboy is already gone. The front gate was left wide open, and the front door was still unlocked as well," Dante told Alinna. "We're looking the place over, but I'm pretty sure that Samuel up and disappeared since he knew we were coming."

"So what now?"

"We're on our way back to the hospital. I wanna talk to both Dominic and Roosevelt. Is Carmen still there?"

Alinna shifted her eyes to Carmen and locked eyes with her.

"Yeah, she's still here."

"I'll talk with her too, once we get there," Dante answered.

"All right!" Alinna replied. "Also, I spoke with Mr. Sutter and Mr. Goldmen. The both of them will be here within the next thirty minutes. I told them that you would be meeting them here to discuss business."

"I'm on my way. Did Monica call you?"

"Yeah. I called Natalie and explained to her what you wanted done with Monica and that Johnson guy."

"All right. He works for us now!"

"Doing what?"

"I'll explain later when I see you."

Alinna hung up the phone and announced to the others what Dante had explained to her about Samuel Randolph, and that he and the others were on their way back to the hospital.

"What did Dante want with me?" Carmen asked, drawing Alinna's eyes back to her.

Alinna easily noticed that the woman was nervous about something. She slowly smirked and then answered Carmen's question, "Dante said that he would speak with you when he got back here."

SEVEN

MONICA RETURNED TO JOHNSON'S office at his request, after he mentioned that he had something he wanted to show her.

Monica stood behind Johnson as he sat in front of his laptop and clicked away at a few keys. He then turned the screen so that she could see.

"Who the hell is Samuel Thorpe?" she asked, reading the information on the man.

She was surprised to find out that Thorpe was a retired FBI agent.

"Why are you showing me this?" Monica asked after she was finished reading.

"It was something Dante said earlier," he replied, smiling at Monica. "I didn't think about it at first, but on the way back it came to me."

"No! Why?"

"Never mind!" Johnson said. "Listen, Monica. This is the same guy who Dante is looking for. I know because I remember some years back when I was just starting out with the DEA that there was a huge investigation about a senior FBI agent by the name of Samuel Thorpe, who was supposedly the half-brother of the drug lord Edward Randolph. It was later found out that Samuel Thorpe had changed his name from Samuel Randolph."

"Why didn't the FBI first catch on when Thorpe joined the organization?"

"It was never figured out," Johnson told her. "Samuel Thorpe resigned from his position and just disappeared."

"But the computer says that he retired."

"Thorpe was pretty high up in the ranks, and instead of putting out that he basically quit or that the FBI fired him, it was said that he retired."

"And you're sure this is the same guy?"

Turning the screen back to face him, Johnson hit a few more keys and then turned the screen back toward Monica.

"That's the guy right there!"

Monica stared at the picture of a surprisingly handsome older man.

She took out her cell phone and said, "Make me a print of this, Nash!"

* * *

Dante heard his cell phone ring while he, Alinna, Dominic, Carmen, Roosevelt, and Evelyn sat discussing new business orders and deals with both Mr. Sutter and Mr. Goldmen, who Dante introduced as new members of the Council Covenant.

When he saw that Monica was on the phone, he held up a finger for the others to hold on as he stepped away and answered, "Yeah, Monica."

"Dante, where are you?"

"At the hospital with Dominic and Alinna. Why?"

"I just got some information that Nash found out on Samuel Randolph. You're not going to believe what he showed me!"

"You on your way here now?"

"Right now!"

"I'ma talk to you when you get here."

After he hung up the phone and returned to the group, Dante caught Alinna's eyes a moment. He said nothing and instead turned back to the conversation that was going on.

"What's the decision gonna to be?" Dante asked, directing the question to Dominic and Roosevelt.

Dominic stared at his son-in-law for a moment and then looked over at Roosevelt, with whom he met eyes and a slight nod of the head.

Dominic then looked back at Dante and said, "All right, Dante, we'll agree to the terms of the deal you've offered. But understand that we're only doing this because we're both aware of the enemies we'll be up against once the product is released onto the streets, and I'm sure everyone inside this room is fully aware of what you're capable of handling. So again, we'll agree to the terms that were set."

Dante nodded his head toward Dominic and then looked at both Mr. Sutter and Mr. Goldmen, who stood quietly and simply nodded their approval as well.

Dante then looked back at Dominic and said, "When can we meet with this Kevin Kim?"

"There's a meeting set up for next week—on Monday!" Roosevelt spoke up, drawing everyone's attention to him. "A phone call will need to be made to inform Mr. Kim of your joining us at the meeting."

Nodding his head in agreement, Dante looked over to Alinna and asked, "You have anything you want to say?"

"You've covered everything," she replied, shaking her head no.

"Dante, if this meeting is over, I'd like to speak with you in private, please," Carmen asked him, staring straight at her son-in-law.

Dante nodded his head, said a few more words to Mr. Sutter and Mr. Goldmen, and then turned back to Carmen and followed her into the hall.

"We'll be back!" Dante told Carlos and the others.

Carlos motioned for two of his men to follow behind Dante and Carmen.

"Dante, I think I need to explain."

"Carmen, you don't have to explain anything to me," Dante told her, cutting her off before she could finish what she was trying to say to him.

"Whatever happens or was going on before I got here to Phoenix was then, but I trust you. You wouldn't have had me come out here if you were playing for the opposite team. And before you mention it, what happened in the restroom will remain in the restroom!"

Carmen stared up into her son-in-law's eyes and slowly shook her head. She wrapped her arms around his waist and laid her head on his chest.

* * *

Monica arrived back at the hospital and rushed to get back onto the floor where Dante's father-in-law was located. She stepped off the elevator just as Dante and Carmen were walking past the elevator.

"Dante!"

Recognizing Monica's voice, Dante stopped and turned around to face her as she left the elevator and walked over to join him and Carmen.

Dante spoke first, seeing the cream-colored folder in her hand: "That's the information you said

Johnson found?"

Monica handed the folder to Dante and stated, "You remember the name we first gave you— Samuel Randolph? Well, that's the birth name, but it was changed to Samuel Thorpe."

"Samuel Thorpe?" Carmen asked, looking from Monica to Dante. "What is she talking about, Dante?"

"From what these papers say, Samuel Atlas's real name is Samuel D. Randolph, but it was changed to Samuel C. Thorpe. He worked for the FBI until retiring a few years ago after it was discovered that he was related to Edward Randolph. He then disappeared after he retired, and was never heard from again."

"Because he changed his name to Samuel T. Atlas and joined the Council Covenant," Monica added, drawing Carmen's attention to her. "So, what happened when you all went after him, Dante?"

"He disappeared again!" Dante admitted. "But that's where I need you and Johnson to get to work. Start with Edward Randolph! Find out where he rests his head at, and find out who's all tied in with this dude and then get me their addresses or locations."

"I'll get with Nash," Monica replied. "You need anything else?"

"Yeah, see if Johnson knows anyone that deals with armor."

"I want to get Dominic, Carmen, Roosevelt, Alinna, and Natalie's cars all bulletproofed," Dante explained, just as he heard Alinna calling his name.

Dante turned around and looked back up the hall as Alinna was rushing toward him. He started toward his wife and called, "What's up? What happened?"

"It's Zoe Papi!" Alinna told him, holding out her cell phone to him. "It's about Rob!"

Dante grabbed the phone from her, placed the cell phone to his ear, and said, "Yeah!"

"What's up, killa? I have a little information for you."

"I'm listening."

"Remember the boy Rob you was looking for before you and Alinna left town? Well, I know where the boy lays his head at now!"

"What about Fish Man?"

"That I don't know. But if you wish me to, I'll have the boy Rob picked up and—!"

"Nah!" Dante interrupted. "You've done what was asked, and I'll have your money, but I want you to keep an eye on Rob for me. We'll be there soon to deal with him."

"Whatever you say!"

Dante hung up the phone, handed it back to Alinna, and then said, "He's got a location on Rob."

"So what are we gonna do?" she asked him.

"We deal with this meeting with this Japanese connect, and then afterward we'll make a trip back home to deal with Rob."

"Dante, what about what's going on here?" Monica asked him.

"Dante, after the meeting with Mr. Kim, why don't me, the girls, and some security guards take a trip out to Miami and deal with Rob. Then once we're done, we'll fly back. That way, you can handle what's going on here."

Dante stared into Alinna's eyes with a negative response on the tip of his tongue, but he knew how his wife would react if he rejected what she was asking.

Instead, he looked at Monica and said, "Tell Johnson I want another vest for Alinna!"

"Vest?" Alinna asked with a confused look on her face as she stared at Dante.

"Bulletproof vest, Alinna!" Monica answered for Dante.

* * *

"What's up with Carmen?" Alinna asked as she and Dante were driving home after finally leaving the hospital.

He turned his head and looked over at Alinna, who was waiting for him to answer her question.

Dante then focused back on the road but said, "She was still messing around with Samuel, but I don't think it was sexual this time. I just think she was just at that point of being comfortable and trusting with the nigga."

"So basically what you're saying is that Carmen's the reason why Edward Randolph knows about the new heroin connect that Dominic and Roosevelt know about?"

Dante nodded his head as he came to a stop at a red light.

He then looked back over at Alinna and said, "I honestly think Carmen was somewhat in love with or had deep feelings for Samuel. She didn't expect homeboy to be the one who would cross the Council Covenant, or specifically her, this way."

Alinna remained quiet for a moment as Dante pulled off once the light turned green.

She looked over at him and asked, "So, what's your plan to deal with Samuel and his brother?"

"I'm killing them both!" Dante stated, looking over toward Alinna again. "I'ma murder both their asses and every muthafucka that's part of that organization. Period!"

Not surprised in the least by her husband's answer, and with nothing more to say about the subject, Alinna reached over and took Dante's right hand into hers. She intertwined their fingers as she laid their hands on her lap. She then turned her attention out the passenger window and allowed her mind to wander on to thoughts of Miami and dealing with Rob and hopefully Fish Man.

EIGHT

AFTER DOMINIC WAS FINALLY released from the hospital, he, Dante, Alinna, Roosevelt, James, and two new bodyguards assigned to Dominic and Roosevelt made the flight from Phoenix to Honshu, Japan.

Once they landed early the next morning, a day after leaving the States, Dante was the first off the G4 jet. He instantly locked in on the Mercedes limo and Mercedes truck that were waiting for them on the airstrip.

"That's Yasmine Kim," Dominic informed Dante, who noticed the slim yet athletic and muscular young Asian woman with straight, long black hair in a ponytail that cascaded over her right shoulder.

"So, she's Mr. Kim's daughter, huh?" Dante asked while watching the team of Asian security moving into position on each side of the young woman.

Dante waited for Alinna at the bottom of the steps. He allowed Dominic and Roosevelt to walk ahead of him with their new bodyguards, who were introduced to the group by James. Wayne was assigned to Dominic, while Jackson was assigned to

Roosevelt. Dante and James then both escorted Alinna over to the others.

"Miss Kim, meet Mr. Dante Blackwell and his wife, Alinna Blackwell. I spoke with your father about them joining us as business partners," Dominic introduced while leaning most of his weight on his pearl and gold walking cane.

"Mr. Blackwell," Yasmine said in perfect English.

She bowed slightly to Dante and then repeated the same routine with Alinna, all while keeping an intrigued eye on Dante.

"Shall we leave?" she asked as one of her men opened the back door to the limo.

"Is Mr. Kim inside?" Dante asked before anyone with him moved toward the limo to get inside.

"I will be taking you all to him, Mr. Blackwell," Yasmine answered, watching Dante very closely.

She caught the shift in his eyes while the party with him all stood waiting and watching his decision. She saw his slightest head nod as the first white male on the left side of Alinna moved forward and climbed into the back of the limo.

Yasmine then saw Dante usher Alinna into the back of the limo, and met Dante's eyes as he then climbed inside behind her. Yasmine Kim smiled slightly as she watched him duck his head when he stepped inside.

Dante, Alinna, James, Dominic, Roosevelt, and Yasmine rode in the limo while Wayne and Jackson followed closely behind them in the truck. Alinna noticed the way the Japanese woman was eyeing Dante.

"Where exactly is Mr. Kim?" Dante spoke first, breaking the silence.

"My father had other business that had to be taken care of," she replied. "He sent me in his place to greet all of you. Am I not good enough, Mr. Blackwell?"

"It was simply a question, Miss Kim!" Dante replied, looking from his window over to meet Yasmine Kim's stare.

The limousine entered a jungle-like area about ten minutes later. Dante sat staring out the tinted window at all the tall trees and whatever else was moving around out there. The limo continued driving through the trail that was in the middle of the jungle, until it reached an opening and the foliage faded away. Dante sat up and stared at what appeared to be a castle at the top of the hill.

"So this is how they live out here, huh?" Alinna said while leaning against Dante and looking out the window next to him.

Yasmine made her presence known to four guards by calling out in Japanese once the limousine pulled up in front of a tall, black-painted gate. A moment later, the gate doors swung open and the limo pulled inside the complex toward the castle-like mansion.

Dante stared out the window and saw armed guards positioned all over the property. He then nodded his head in approval at how security was set up. After the limo was parked and the chauffeur opened up the back door, Yasmine was the first one out while the others followed.

"This guy must be the president of Japan or something!" Alinna said to Dante, after climbing from the back of the limo and looking around.

Dante didn't respond to Alinna's comment. Instead, he simply focused on the team of four guards who were standing at the open front door of the mansion. Dante laid his left hand on the small of Alinna's back and guided her behind Yasmine as James followed alongside Alinna. Both Dominic and Roosevelt followed with their bodyguards.

Dante stepped inside the mansion once the guards shifted away from blocking the doorway. He then looked around the three-story mansion, only to shift his eyes toward the two guards who stepped in front of him, Alinna, and James.

"What the—" Alinna started, stepping back as one of the guards reached out for her breast, only for Dante's hand to shoot out and grab hold of the guard's wrist.

Seconds later, James smashed a kick to the guard's midsection that sent him flying backward across the floor.

Yasmine was surprised at what she had just witnessed, yet intrigued by what she was watching. She locked her eyes onto Dante as he and the white male worked perfectly together while keeping Alinna protected.

"Enough!"

Yasmine recognized her father's voice. She tore her eyes away from Dante to look over at her father as he stood at the top of the stairs, surrounded by his two personal bodyguards. Yasmine walked over to the bottom of the stairwell as her father began making his way down.

Dante watched as the middle-aged Japanese man and his bodyguards walked down the stairs. He was sure he was seeing Kevin Kim for the first time. He then shifted his eyes toward the guards with whom he and James had the altercation as they all scurried away when their boss reached the bottom stair.

"Dominic Saldana! Fredrick Roosevelt!" Kim began.

He then looked at Dante, Alinna, and James and continued, "I assume that these three belong with the Blackwell family I was told would be joining us for this business meeting. Correct?"

"You're correct!" Dante spoke up as he then introduced himself, Alinna, and James to Mr. Kim.

"Would you mind telling me exactly why you attacked my guards?" Kevin Kim asked.

Mr. Kim then heard his daughter speak up from behind where he was standing: "Father, I am responsible for the misunderstanding. I didn't warn Mr. Blackwell that he and his people would be searched. Dan . . . I mean Mr. Blackwell and the other gentleman were only protecting Mrs. Blackwell."

Nodding his head and then turning his attention back to Dante Blackwell and the others, Kevin Kim gave a smile and then said, "My apologies, Mr. and Mrs. Blackwell. Please excuse my guards. Shall we move this meeting along?"

Nodding his head in response to Mr. Kim, Dante started behind the Japanese drug lord, with Alinna at his side and James on the opposite side of her.

He looked to Yasmine Kim and caught her watching him. He nodded his head in thanks and was rewarded with a small smile before she responded with a slight bow.

NINE

THE GROUP SPENT TWO more days with the Kims than were planned. They not only discussed business, but they were also shown around Japan and even stopped to see the warehouse filled with Kim's heroin workers. Dante took in everything that was told to him and paid close attention to what was shown to him and the others as well.

On the morning of the flight back to the States, Mr. Kim rode out to the airstrip with his guests to see them off and to discuss a few last-minute details. Once the limo pulled to a stop in front of Dominic's G4 jet, Mr. Kim was the first to exit. He was met by an even larger than normal team of bodyguards.

While saying their goodbyes, Mr. Kim stopped Dante before he could leave, and said, "Dante, before you leave, I think my daughter would like to have a word with you."

Dante looked at Yasmine as Mr. Kim stepped away. He watched the Japanese woman step forward, stopping in front of him.

She took off the gold chain that hung around her neck, and with two hands she offered it to Dante and said, "Mr. Blackwell, I respect you as a man of great power and strength, but most of all for the great warrior I see that you are. Please accept this gift I have to offer to you, and know that I am yours to command. Will you accept this gift I offer only to you?"

Dante looked down at the chain with the heart charm that had two swords crossed over the front of the heart. He remembered that Yasmine wore earrings with the same design. As Dante looked back at her as she stood with her head down, he noticed that Mr. Kim watched him closely with a serious expression on his face.

Dante took the chain from Yasmine's hands and said, "I accept your gift, Yasmine, and thank you."

"This is wonderful," Mr. Kim cried out as he clapped his hands, pulled Dante into a fatherly embrace, and then hugged his daughter and kissed her cheek.

"Dante!" Dominic called out as he stepped beside his son-in-law. "Son, do you know much about Japanese customs and beliefs?"

"Nothing really. Why?" Dante asked, seeing the smirk on Dominic's face.

Roosevelt walked up to him with a smile and said, "Congratulations!"

"Congratulations for what?" Alinna asked with a confused look on her face.

"Your husband just accepted Yasmine Kim as yet another wife," Roosevelt said, laughing as he walked off and headed toward the jet.

Dante looked over at Dominic and saw his father-in-law nodding his head in approval at the unasked question. He then looked over at both Yasmine and Mr. Kim, and he was surprised to see six of Kim's guards holding luggage and waiting on Yasmine.

Yasmine looked over at Dante and smiled at him.

She hugged her father, walked over and stood beside Dante, and said, "I'm ready when you are, my husband."

* * *

Once all of them got on the jet and were on their way back to Arizona. Dante found himself dealing with Alinna's attitude while listening to Yasmine break down the customs. Dante then realized that he and Yasmine were, in fact, now married according to Japanese beliefs, because of the gold chain that he accepted and wore around his neck.

"My husband, are you upset about something?" Yasmine asked, noticing the look on Dante's face.

Dante shook his head and told her that he would be right back as he disappeared into the back of the plane to a bedroom.

"Dante, I don't even want to talk right now!"

Alinna told him as soon as she saw him enter the room.

Dante ignored her and closed the sliding door behind him. He then walked around to the bedside where Alinna sat, and he sat down beside her. Alinna immediately stood up and walked away.

"Alinna, come here, shorty! You seriously wanna be heated with me about this shit when I didn't know shit about what was going on?"

Alinna opened her mouth to yell at him, but she was unable to really fault him when she knew for a fact that, like her, he knew nothing about what was going on when Yasmine offered him the gold necklace.

Alinna slowly shook her head, sighed loudly and deeply, and said, "Why is it that women keep tying themselves to you wherever your ass goes, nigga?"

"What do you want me to say?"

Alinna shook her head at Dante again and asked, "So now I guess you want me to accept this one as your wife too? I gotta share you with another woman, huh, Dante?"

Just as he was about to speak, Dante heard a soft knock on the door. He then heard Yasmine's voice call out to Alinna. Dante sat watching as Alinna walked over to the door, unlocked it, and then slid open the door to see Yasmine standing there.

"May I speak with you and Dante a moment, Alinna?" Yasmine asked, meeting and holding Alinna's eyes.

Sighing and stepping to the side, Alinna motioned Yasmine inside the bed chambers and then closed and locked the door behind her.

Yasmine looked from Dante to Alinna as she stood next to the door with her arms folded across her chest.

Yasmine then began, "Alinna, I think I understand what is going on and why I see the troubled look on Dante's face. We've spoken of the customs of the Japanese people, and I am aware that you and Dante are married. But in Japan, the men of power are allowed more than one wife. I also understand that you are his first wife, and I will always respect your position as the head beside Dante. All I ask is that you allow me to prove myself and try to accept me into the Blackwell family. I know that this is all so sudden, but in all my twenty years of living, I have never met a man as strong and powerful a warrior as Dante, not even my father, who is one of the most powerful men in all of Japan."

Alinna laughed before she even realized it as she

looked at Dante and said, "I swear to you now, I will not accept one more woman into this family. I don't care how much I love your ass. There isn't that much love or sharing in the world. I will kill you first, Dante!"

Dante saw Alinna's smile but heard the seriousness in her words. He stood up from the bed and walked over to her, only to grab her around the back and grip her ass as he pulled her up against him. He then bent down and kissed his wife on the lips as Alinna wrapped her arms around his neck.

* * *

They landed in Phoenix by the afternoon the next day. Once again, Dante was the first one off the plane, followed by Alinna and Yasmine, then James behind the two women, and the six bodyguards sent with Yasmine.

Dante was not surprised to see Dre, Vanessa, and the rest of the family all waiting as they exited the jet. Dante allowed both Yasmine and Alinna to walk ahead of him as he turned to Yasmine's guards and directed them to follow James over to the Escalade.

"Dante!" Dominic called out as he and Roosevelt walked over to his son-in-law. "We're going to go ahead home. We can all meet up tomorrow to discuss how things are going to be handled as far as business."

"Tomorrow then!" Dante replied as he shook the men's hands.

Dante watched as his father-in-law and Roosevelt were escorted to their limo by security. Dante then turned his attention to Dre, Tony T, Wesley, and a slim but muscular brown-skinned man.

"Who's homeboy?"

"Relax, me brethren!" Wesley spoke up first, smiling at Dante as he made introductions. "Rastaman, this is me rude boy cousin. Me call him Gage. But he name is Doyle Gage."

"What's he doing here, Wesley?" Dante asked while staring straight at Gage.

"I gave Wesley the okay for Gage to come here," Alinna called out from where she stood with Vanessa and the other girls.

Alinna watched as Dante's face slowly balled up as she added, "Gage is now going to be your new bodyguard, and that is what I'm ordering!"

"What the!"

"It's not up for discussion, Dante!" Alinna told him, with a finalized tone to her voice while holding his heated gaze.

Dante stared at Alinna and wanted to say something, but he did not want to go against her in front of the family.

Instead, Dante growled, "Everybody get the fuck in the car!"

Alinna watched her husband angrily walk off and head to the Land Rover with Dre and James, with the rest of the men following behind them.

She then looked to Yasmine and heard her say, "Alinna, are you sure you should have made this decision without discussing it with Mr. Blackwell first?"

"Maybe for one of us it would have been deadly to our very life," Alinna heard Vanessa say, drawing everyone's attention. "What we've all learned is that Dante has the only spot open in his heart for Alinna, Natalie, and his kids, and they are the only ones that can get away with things like what Alinna just got away with."

"Who's Natalie?" Yasmine asked, looking toward Alinna.

"I'm pretty sure I said let's go!" Dante called out as Dre pulled the Land Rover up beside the Mercedes truck that Alinna and the other women stood in front, drawing all of their eyes around to him.

"We're coming!" Alinna replied as she rolled her

eyes at Dante.

Alinna then walked over to the passenger seat front door of the Benz truck, ignoring the way Dante was staring at her from inside the Land Rover.

Alinna left the airstrip and followed behind Dre in the Land Rover. She finally introduced Yasmine to the girls and let them know who she was to Dante. She received a what-the-fuck look from Vanessa, who drove the Benz truck.

From the backseat, Amber said, "Damn! My brother got even Japanese bitches chasing his ass! I guess we got another sister-in-law now, huh?"

"Oh shit!" Vanessa said, remembering something. "Alinna, I forgot to tell Dante that Natalie is at the hospital with Harmony."

"Harmony's having the baby already?" Alinna asked Vanessa with a smile.

"Both Harmony and Natalie about to have their babies soon!" Vanessa told her, seeing the smile slip from Alinna's face. "Both of them started having pains early this morning. Harmony was first. What's crazy was that Natalie was the one that was with Harmony, and she started having pains right after she called Tony T."

"Gimme a phone," Alinna said.

Amber sat forward and handed over her phone to

Alinna and said, "Dante's on the phone, A!"

Taking the phone from Amber, Alinna told Dante what Vanessa just told her, only for Dante to calmly reply, "I already knew, Alinna. Tony T just told me what's up, and that both Harmony and Natalie are all right. We're heading to the hospital now."

* * *

"Yes, sir. May I help you?" Dr. Dori Lewis asked, after seeing the hospital room door open and the extremely handsome young man fly inside.

Breaking out in a huge smile at the sight of Dante, Natalie began to cry as he walked right up to her bedside. She wrapped her arms around his neck as Dante bent down to kiss her.

"How you feeling, beautiful?" Dante asked, smiling down at her once she released him. Dante then gently wiped her tears from her face.

"I'm okay!" Natalie answered, still smiling and happy to see Dante.

"Miss Saldana, is this the baby's father?" Dr. Lewis asked, looking from Dante to Natalie.

After Natalie introduced Dante to her doctor, who promised to return in five minutes to check on her, Natalie turned back to him and said, "You just missed Mother, Dante. She just left with Carlos."

"I noticed the four men outside your room,"

Dante replied as he sat down on the side of the bed.

"Where is everyone?" she asked as she took Dante's hand into hers.

"They stopped by to see about Harmony first, so that I can have some time alone with you."

"I missed you, baby!"

"I missed you too, beautiful."

"How did everything go in Japan?"

Dante nodded his head slowly and then winked at Natalie, which caused her to smile back at him.

He then remembered Yasmine and said, "Natalie, we need to talk, beautiful!"

* * *

"So, you're Dante's new wife, huh?" Harmony asked the Japanese woman who Alinna had just introduced as Yasmine Kim.

"I can't believe this. Dante got three women?" Maxine said as she stood up and hugged James. "Too bad James is my boo, because I would love to be wife number four!"

"Shut up, Maxine!" Keisha told her twin sister while shaking her head.

Alinna was also shaking her head, but she couldn't help but smile when she focused back on Harmony.

She then changed the subject and said, "I've got some good news for all of you! We're leaving for Miami soon."

"What?" Harmony and the other girls all said together as they stared at Alinna with shock and confusion.

Alinna explained to the girls about the phone call from Zoe Papi, and her and Dante's decision to deal with Rob and hopefully Fish Man.

She then looked at Vanessa and heard her ask, "So you telling me that Dante is actually letting you fly back to Miami without him, Alinna?"

Alinna nodded her head yes. She understood why Vanessa and the other girls were surprised that Dante was allowing her to fly back to Miami without him being there.

She continued, "Dante and the rest of the guys are staying here to deal with what's going on here while we head home to deal with problems that should have long been dealt with."

"But isn't that dangerous, Alinna?" Harmony asked. "We're splitting the family in half to try and deal with two different problems. Everybody is here, but if we leave for Miami, then we're taking half. Because even if Dante is allowing you to fly back to

Miami, I'm willing to bet he sends half if not more than half the family with us for backup."

"I may just be able to assist with that problem," Yasmine spoke up, which drew everyone's attention to her. "If security is an issue, then I can have fifty men here or in Miami to assist us with this problem you all spoke of."

"You serious?" Amber asked Yasmine, who simply nodded her head yes.

Alinna heard the door open and saw Dante walk in followed by Dre, Tony T, Wesley, and Gage. She then looked over at Harmony, who happily cried out Dante's name.

"How ya feeling, baby girl?" Dante asked as he stopped beside her bed, bent down, and kissed Harmony's cheek as she tightly hugged his neck.

"Damn! I don't get that kind of love when I show up, and I'm ya man!" Tony T playfully joked, which made everyone laugh and Harmony roll her eyes at him.

"How's my nephew doing?" Dante asked, rubbing Harmony's blanket-covered belly.

Harmony smiled when the baby responded to Dante's touch that moved against her stomach. She then looked up to meet his eyes, and she was happy to see that he had one of his gorgeous smiles showing.

"Well, I'm sorry to disappoint you, God Daddy, but we're having a girl."

Harmony smiled, when all of her girls rushed the bed all talking at once. Harmony admitted that she and Tony T knew what sex the baby was and had decided not to mention it, explaining that she just wanted to let Dante know.

"So, I get another girl to take care of, huh?" Dante replied, rubbing Harmony's stomach, which caused the baby to respond again.

"Well, I can see now that she knows her god daddy!" Harmony said, smiling up at Dante. "She just keeps kicking every time Dante rubs my stomach."

"Damn! First my women, and now my daughter too!" Tony T commented, shaking his head and smiling.

"So, Dante!" Vanessa said, getting his attention. "Alinna was telling us about Zoe Papi calling and telling y'all what's up about Rob."

Dante nodded his head and slowly began to lose his smile at the thought of business.

He said, "Yeah! I want you, Alinna, and the rest

of y'all to fly back to Miami and deal with Rob. I'm sending the crew back with y'all while me, Dre, Tony T, Wesley, and his cousin will deal with everything that's going on up here."

Alinna caught the look that Vanessa shot her and said, "Dante, Yasmine was just telling us that she's going to help us. She's going to have fifty men flown out to Miami to meet us there. I'm going to call ahead and have Greg Wilson have what we need set up for us."

Dante looked over at Yasmine, who nodded her head in agreement to what Alinna just told him.

He then called out to James and said, "You're flying back with them. You know what I need you to do. Protect Alinna and look after Yasmine."

"Not a problem," James answered.

"Mr. Blackwell?" Yasmine said.

"Dante, Yasmine. Call me Dante," he told her.

Yasmine nodded her head in understanding and then said, "Dante, I am fully aware that James is Alinna's personal bodyguard, but if I may request that he be released from his position and allow me to fill in the position as Alinna's personal bodyguard. It will also allow us time to get to know one another."

"Yasmine, I understand that you want to get to know Alinna, but James is trained to—!"

"No disrespect to Mr. Grant, but I do believe that I am better trained than he is, and I am more than capable of protecting Alinna!" Yasmine interrupted him.

Alinna then spoke up and added, "I agree! James, from now on your position is at Dante's side along with Gage! Nothing at all should happen to my husband with the two of you protecting him, even though he is highly able to protect himself. Just make sure you both watch his back, and Yasmine will take over for you, James."

James looked over at Dante for the final say as he saw the look on Dante's face as he stared straight at Alinna.

"Bruh, what's up? What you want me to do?" James asked.

Dante continued to stare straight into Alinna's eyes and replied, "Do exactly what Alinna says."

Alinna slowly smiled at Dante's response. She then walked over to her husband and kissed him lightly on the lips and then whispered, "Thank you!"

TEN

DANTE DEALT WITH BOTH Natalie and Harmony as they gave birth to their babies. Harmony gave Tony T a beautiful girl they agreed to name Crystal Truman, while Natalie gave birth to a son the next day. She and Dante agreed on the name Damian Blackwell, with the middle name of Saldana. Dante and the rest of the Council Covenant then dealt with the shipment that Mr. Kim had sent over three days after the birth of the babies.

One week after the shipment arrived, Alinna and the rest of the girls readied themselves to make the flight out to Miami to deal with unfinished business that was waiting. Dante and the guys rode out to the airstrip with the women.

"Call me when you get to Miami," Dante told Alinna as the two of them stood outside in front of his new Porsche 911 Targa 4 GTS, which was a twin to the Porsche Macan Turbo that he bought for Alinna—both cars armored.

"Relax, Dante!" Alinna told him, sensing the look on his face whenever he worried about her.

She was just about to say more when Mya ran over and pushed in between the two of them to get to her father.

Alinna shook her head and smiled as she stood watching Dante and his daughter. It still amazed her how Mya was able to bring the softness completely out of her husband and how Dante spoiled his daughter. Alinna looked to her right as Yasmine stepped beside her.

"This is a side of Dante that surprises me!" Yasmine stated as she stood watching Dante and his daughter talking to each other.

"Mya is the key to his heart, Yasmine," Alinna told her, looking back to Dante and Mya. "He loves that little girl to death!"

Alinna watched as Mya rushed off to catch up with Dante Jr. and Andre Jr., who were following Vanessa and Amber to the jet along with Dre and Wesley. Alinna looked at Dante as he stepped up in front of her and Yasmine.

"Yasmine, I'm expecting you to make sure that security is tight once you all get to Miami," Dante told her in all seriousness, but then added, "Alinna isn't the only one I want protected. When I get to Miami, you two better be how I'm seeing you now!"

Yasmine smiled at his words, bowed her head slightly, and said, "I've spoken with Alinna, and we both have agreed that I will leave you the six guards my father assigned to me. They have their orders and will do as you order them. They are trained to handle deadly issues such as the one you are dealing with now."

Dante shifted his eyes over toward the six Japanese guards that stood a few feet away at ease but were fully alert while still relaxed. Dante then looked back to Yasmine, meeting her dark eyes.

He nodded his head in acceptance and said, "I'll see you two soon."

Alinna kissed her husband after Yasmine hugged and kissed his cheek. Alinna then turned, and both she and Yasmine started toward the jet as Dre, Wesley, Tony T, and James walked out to join Dante.

Dre stopped in front of her and said, "You be safe. Don't have me and Dante fly back to Miami and cause the whole city to get shut down behind something happening to you!"

Alinna smiled at Dre and hugged her brother.

She then hugged a smiling James, who whispered into her ear, "I'll look after Dante. Just promise me you'll stay safe until we get to Miami."

"I promise, James," she told him.

After kissing him on the cheek, she and Yasmine started again for the jet but stopped and called out to Dre.

"Yeah!"

"I forgot to tell Dante. Let him know that his sister made it safely to Syracuse, but that she called and told me that she's meeting us in Miami."

After receiving a nod of the head of understanding from Dre, Alinna turned and followed Yasmine up and onto the jet.

Once on the G4, Alinna took a seat beside Vanessa, who had her nephew, Dante Jr., in her lap and rubbing his curly hair. Yasmine sat directly across from her next to Maxine, who sat staring out the window. Alinna then looked out the window as well and saw Dre, Tony T, Gage, James, and Wesley crowded around Dante as he spoke to them.

"A, relax!" Harmony told Alinna, noticing the look on her sister's face while holding her daughter, Crystal, after receiving her from Emmy. "Dante and them are gonna be fine! How many times have Tony T, Dre, and Dante left the state to handle their business and returned home the same way they left?"

"Think about it!" Vanessa added. "Now the three of them got both James and Wesley, and we all know how those two get down."

"Dante also has Gage," Amber added.

"What's up with Gage?" Harmony asked, looking at Amber.

"Gage is out of the army," Amber told her. "Both

he and Wesley were born here in the States, but spent most of their childhood in Jamaica until they were brought here to live. Gage went into the army and became Special Forces while Wesley became a hustler."

"So, Gage knows that stuff Dante knows then, huh?" Keisha asked.

"I've seen him fight, and he's not as good as Dante, but he specializes with different types of guns and explosives," Amber explained, smiling as she spoke, remembering the demonstrations that Gage put on for her and Wesley after he left the army.

Alinna heard her girls talking but really didn't pay much attention to what they were saying, since her mind was heavy with thoughts of Dante for some reason. Alinna then tried to clear her mind of those thoughts, looking up only to meet Yasmine's dark eyes as she sat watching her closely.

* * *

Dante sat in the front passenger seat of the Porsche while Gage drove and James sat in the back. Dante listened to Monica tell him a little of what she and Nash Johnson found on Edward Randolph as Gage had the Porsche flying away from the airstrip.

Dante hung up with Monica after agreeing to meet her back at the mansion. He then called Dominic's personal number.

"Saldana!"

"Dominic, it's Dante! I'll be at the mansion later on. I've got to meet with somebody and handle something first."

"That's fine. I've also begun dealing with buyers and so forth."

"Let both Roosevelt and Carmen know that I wanna speak with them too, when I get there."

Dante spoke with Dominic a few moments longer before hanging up. He then called Mr. Goldmen and Mr. Sutter to check and make sure that their shipments were delivered to them.

Dante arrived back at the mansion and saw Monica's Jaguar parked in front of the house. He was the first out of the Porsche once Gage parked the car, with James right behind him as they headed to the front door.

"Dante!" Natalie said, smiling at the sight of her husband as she was exiting the kitchen carrying baby Damian.

"Where's Monica?" he asked after Natalie kissed him.

"Both Monica and that Nash Johnson guy are

inside the den with Gomez," Natalie replied.

As James was taking Damian out of her arms, she called to Dante as he began walking away.

"Yeah?"

"Me and mother were thinking. With everything that's going on, maybe me and Damian should go and stay with her until you're ready to leave for Miami."

Dante remained quiet for a few moments thinking over what Natalie had suggested.

He then nodded his approval and said, "All right. Move with your parents, but make sure you call me if anything happens or you need me!"

Natalie smiled as she walked over to Dante, kissed his lips, and said, "I love you!"

Dante smirked while watching Natalie as she took the baby from Dre, who had taken the boy from James. Dante then turned away as his wife started toward the bedroom.

"That boy looks just like yo' ass, fam!" Dre told Dante as he, Dante, and the rest of the men followed Dante into the den.

Once in the den, Dante saw Monica and Johnson talking. Gomez sat barely watching the television, since he was too busy watching Monica.

"Dante!" Monica said, seeing him and the other Blackwell men enter the den.

She took the file that she and Johnson had been looking over, handed it to him, and said, "Read this!"

Dante took the file and remained standing beside Monica's seat on the couch. He then began reading through it and found that it belonged to a man named Victor Elijah. Dante continued to read the information, which was nothing more than the background history on a thirty-eight-year-old drug lord.

"Who's this guy supposed to be, and why do I care?" Dante asked, looking up from the file and over toward Monica.

"Because," Johnson began, drawing Dante's attention to him. "Victor Elijah is a known associate of Edward Randolph. I figure since we've looked deep and long for whomever it is that ties in with Edward Randolph, only to turn up with nothing, you could maybe get Victor Elijah to tell you what we are trying to find out."

"Basically what you're saying is that we find this Victor guy and force the information outta him?" James asked.

"Not find!" Monica said as she pulled out a folded piece of yellow writing paper and handed it to Dante. "That's Victor Elijah's address to his mansion in eastern Arizona. So now all you gotta do is get the information we need!"

Dante looked down at the piece of paper that Monica had handed him. He studied the information on the paper and then pushed it over to James. He then looked back at Monica and Johnson.

Dante then stated, "Good work! But one more thing! We gonna need more fireworks to party with!"

"Not a problem," Johnson replied, smiling at Dante while rubbing both his hands together.

ELEVEN

ALINNA ONLY SLEPT A few minutes on the flight from Phoenix to Miami. She watched as the G4 began its descent after the pilot announced that they were landing. She waited until the jet came to a halt and the hatch opened, before she stood from her seat with Dante Jr. asleep in her arms.

She saw Greg Wilson standing beside her Rolls-Royce Phantom as soon as she stepped off of the jet and began walking down the steps. Alinna then noticed four black Cadillac Escalades and the two Mercedes-Benz trucks parked on the other side of the Phantom.

"I see you and Dante made new friends," Wilson said to Alinna as she and the group of women stopped in front of him.

He then nodded his head back toward the four Escalades and two Benz trucks and said, "I bought one of the Benz trucks as you asked, but the other five SUVs are filled with some Japanese dudes."

"Yasmine!" Alinna called out.

As Alinna looked over at her, she received a bow of the head before Yasmine stepped away from the group and started toward the Escalades and Benz trucks.

"Who's the Japanese woman?" Greg Wilson asked, staring hard at Yasmine's five foot five, slim but toned and muscular, curvy, 34B-26-37 body.

"Careful, Wilson!" Alinna warned. "I'm sure Dante would feel some type of way about you staring at his wife like that!"

Wilson swung his head around to look at Alinna with an expression of disbelief on his face. He asked, "You're joking, right? Dante has another wife?"

"You plan on giving us the keys to the truck, Wilson?" Alinna asked him while holding out her hand and ignoring the question he asked her.

Wilson handed over the keys to the metallic-gray Benz truck.

He then handed an envelope to Alinna and said, "That's for Dante. Tell him it's a birthday gift."

"What's in it?" Alinna asked as Wilson started toward his pearl-white Cadillac Deville, only for the investigator to call back over his shoulder to Alinna: "It's something he asked me about some time ago."

Alinna first looked at Wilson as he climbed into his car, and then back down at the envelope.

She found herself wondering exactly what was inside, when from over her shoulder Amber asked, "You gonna open it, A-girl?"

"No, she's not!" Vanessa answered for Alinna. "It's a birthday gift for Dante."

"I didn't even know it was my boo's birthday!" Harmony said with a smile. "I gotta get my baby a gift for his birthday."

"Yeah! When is Dante's birthday anyway?" Amber asked.

Alinna ignored all of them and handed the keys to the Benz truck to Vanessa, and called to Rose and Emmy, who had the kids. She then turned to her personal armed driver who flew with them, and nodded for him to open the back door of the Phantom for Rose and Emmy.

"We'll drop off the kids, Rose, and Emmy at the house," Alinna told the girls as both housekeepers climbed inside the Rolls-Royce. "Afterward, we'll hook up with Zoe Papi and find out where Rob is at!"

"What about Rafael?"

"What about him?" Harmony asked as she handed Crystal over to Emmy.

"Isn't he still holding Angela's husband, Geno, for Dante?" Amber asked, looking over at Alinna.

Alinna had forgotten about Geno but stated, "I'll call Dante and find out what he wants to do about Geno. Right now, we've got business to handle!"

* * *

Zoe Papi received a phone call from Alinna informing him that she was back in Miami. He agreed to meet with her at one of his trap houses out in Little Haiti. Zoe Papi left for the meeting and rode in his chauffeured Mercedes E-Class Benz with his lieutenant.

Zoe Papi saw Jean Paul's 325I BWM as soon as his E-Class pulled up in front of the trap house. He watched his lieutenant leave the front porch where a few men and some workers stood watching Jean Paul walking out to the Benz. He pulled out a pre-rolled blunt as the chauffeur opened the back door and Jean Paul climbed inside.

"What's up, Zoe Papi?" Jean Paul said as the driver closed the car door. "What you need me to handle, boss?"

"You still got that kid out there watching the boy Rob?" Zoe Papi asked as he blew a cloud of thick weed smoke.

"You never gave me the word to move 'im, so he's still on the Rob guy," Jean Paul answered, just as Zoe Papi dug out his cell phone and stared down at the screen.

He read the text that just had come through from Alinna.

He then slid the phone back into his pocket as he looked over at Jean Paul and ordered, "Call the young kid and find out exactly where Rob is, because he has visitors."

"You mean Dante's back?"

"I said visitors, not Death himself!" Zoe Papi told his lieutenant.

While staring at Jean Paul and seeing the understanding slowly creep into his eyes, Zoe Papi added, "Alinna Blackwell and her girls are back in Miami!"

"She's just as bad!" Jean Paul started, but paused, seeing the neighborhood streets light up as if the sun was rising back into the sky.

Zoe Papi stared out the back tinted window and watched as an Escalade made its way up the street, followed by a second Escalade and the Benz. Zoe Papi slowly smiled as he recognized the Rolls-Royce Phantom that made its way up the street with a second Benz truck following behind.

"What the fuck!" Jean Paul said, staring out the back window at the two Escalades that were now blocking the opposite end of the street.

Zoe Papi turned in his seat and looked out the back window to see what Jean Paul was talking about. He looked back outside again just as the doors opened to the Escalades next to the Phantom and out poured a team of suit-wearing Asian men, some carrying semiautomatic rifles.

"What in the hell?" he said out loud to himself.

He then looked at the Phantom, just as a slim but sexy Asian female climbed from the backseat.

"Who the hell!" Jean Paul started, but then stopped once he saw Alinna Blackwell climb from the backseat of the Phantom. "Ain't this a bitch! It's Alinna!"

Zoe Papi smiled a bit as he lightly tapped the window announcing to the chauffeur that he was ready to get out. He then climbed from the back of his E-Class after his door was opened for him.

"The queen has returned!" Zoe Papi said with a big smile.

However, his smile quickly froze as the path between him and Alinna was instantly blocked by more than ten Asians who all had guns and looked ready to use them.

"Yasmine!" Alinna called as Yasmine spoke in Japanese, causing the guards to step aside and clear the path between her and Zoe Papi.

"I'm impressed!" Zoe Papi said, smiling again as Alinna and the Asian woman walked over to him. "Who's your new friend?"

"Where's Rob and Fish Man?" Alinna asked, ignoring the question.

Zoe Papi smiled wider and looked behind him at Jean Paul. He also noticed the look on the faces of all the men who worked for him who were standing a few feet behind.

"Jean Paul, come over here!" Zoe Papi ordered.

Alinna watched as Jean Paul made his way over to stand beside Zoe Papi. Alinna then returned the nod that she received from the lieutenant.

"Where is Rob at now?" Zoe Papi asked Jean Paul.

"My guy Edwin says he's at his trap spot over in Brown Sub!" Jean Paul answered, looking back over toward Alinna as he spoke.

"What's the address?" she asked, holding Jean Paul's eyes.

* * *

"So what are you planning to do, Dante?" Carmen asked as she, Dre, Dominic, and Roosevelt all sat inside Dominic's home office, with both Mr. Sutter and Mr. Goldmen on the speaker phone.

"Well, right now I've got James and Tony T driving out to eastern Arizona looking into the address we have," Dante began as he pulled out his ringing phone to see that Kerri Cook was calling him.

Dante told the others to hold on and walked from the office while answering the phone, "Yeah, Kerri. What's up, shorty?"

"Hi, Dante. Alinna asked me to call you and let you know that we all made it to Miami."

"Where is she now?"

"Left with the others to go and handle the business we came back for. I'm on my way to pick up your sister from the motel she's staying at."

"Kerri, make sure you check out Melody from that motel and tell her I want her at the house with everyone else, and also assign two guards to her! Matter of fact, take her to pick out a car."

"I'll take care of it, Dante!" Kerri told him, but then asked, "How's everything going out there with you all?"

"It's about to get real-lived out here, shorty! But let me get back in this meeting. Tell Alinna to call me when she gets home or gets some free time."

* * *

Rob stepped outside onto the front porch of the apartment that he used for a trap house. He was followed by his right-hand man who he hired as his gunman since the beef with Dante and Alinna Blackwell really jumped off. He knew that the Blackwells had left Miami and left power in the hands of Rafael, the crazy Jamaican. As such, Rob still wanted to stay on point just in case anything else was to jump off.

Rob's cell phone rang just as he was saying a few last-minute words to his workers. He nodded to them as he dug out his phone and walked off the porch.

Rob saw that Fish Man was calling him. He started to answer the call when his gunman grabbed his arm before he stepped out the front gate. He looked up and over at his gunman, but his attention quickly turned toward the street, when he saw his gunman's face staring in that direction.

"You expecting company?" the gunman asked Rob.

They watched as two Escalade trucks and a Benz truck pulled up in front of the trap house.

"Hell no!" Rob answered, staring at the three SUVs, only to see two more Escalades and another Benz truck pull up from the opposite end of the street. "What the hell!"

Rob felt his gunman grab his arm and pull him backward at the same time the driver's and back doors opened. Rob was surprised to see Vanessa and Tony T's lady, Harmony, climb from the truck.

"What's up, Rob?" Vanessa called out, smirking at Rob as she and Harmony closed the truck doors.

Keisha, Maxine, and Amber walked around from the other side of the truck.

"What the hell are y'all doing here?" Rob asked, noticing the look on Keisha's face. "I heard y'all left town!"

"Well, we decided to come back!" Vanessa replied, but then said, "Somebody wants to talk with you."

"Naw, I'm good!"

"That wasn't a request, nigga!" Keisha spoke up, spitting her words at Rob. "You either come with us or we're just going to snatch yo punk ass up!"

Rob slowly smiled as his gunman smoothly pulled his banger from his waist. Rob saw Vanessa pull out her phone and make a phone call. He watched the he-she bitch until she hung up, and then noticed a smirk appear on her lips.

"Today's your lucky day!" Vanessa told him. "We can handle this right here."

"Handle what?" Rob asked, just as something caught his attention from the corner of his left eye.

He felt his heart speed up at the familiar sight of the Rolls-Royce Phantom that was pulling up behind the Benz truck out of which Vanessa and the others exited.

Rob watched the driver climb out and walk to the back and open the door. He was confused when he saw the Asian woman climb out. He then swung his attention over to the four Escalades and saw suit-wearing Asian men with big toys in their hands climb out.

"How's it going, Rob?"

Rob recognized the Spanish-accented voice and looked over at the Phantom. Alinna was standing beside the Asian woman, who was now gripping a Beretta 9mm in her right hand against her thigh.

"Alinna, what are you doing here? Where's Dante?" he asked.

"Worry about what's happening now, Rob!" Alinna told him. "I need some answers, and you're going to give them to me! Let's go!"

"He's not going!"

Boom! Boom!

Rob barely saw the Asian woman when she moved her right hand that held a Beretta. He looked to his right as his gunman stumbled backward, dropped his banger, and grabbed his chest that was pumping blood across his front. Rob then watched his gunman as he fell to his knees trying to breathe.

Boom!

Rob jumped away from his gunman after seeing his face blown open. He then looked back at a now-smiling Alinna while the Asian woman calmly stood beside her, staring her dark-colored eyes at him.

"Are you ready to go now, Rob?" Alinna asked, still smiling at him.

TWELVE

VICTOR ELIJAH CLIMBED FROM his limousine once the chauffeur parked and opened his door, and he started toward the front door of his mansion. His cell phone rang just as his front door slowly swung open. He saw that it was his wife calling. He then looked inside the door and stared straight at a handsome young man, with gold teeth staring at him.

"Who the hell are you?" Victor asked, both confused and with growing anger. "How the hell did you get into my house?"

"You may wanna answer your phone!" the stranger calmly told Victor, in a voice that was just louder than a whisper.

Victor first looked at the man in his house and then down at his phone, and then answered, "Oliva!" Hearing his wife scream out his name right before the line went dead, Victor looked back at the stranger.

"Oliva is fine for the moment, Victor. How long she stays that way is up to you!" the stranger informed.

"Who the fuck are you?" Victor asked angrily as he walked up to the stranger. "What the hell do you even want?"

"Edward Randolph and everybody that has any type of business dealing with him," the stranger told him, staring the drug lord directly into his eyes.

Victor slowly nodded his head in understanding, and with a calmer voice said, "You're Dante Blackwell, right? Dominic Saldana's son-in-law, correct?"

"I take it Samuel Atlas, I mean Samuel Randolph must have told you about me?" Dante asked him.

"The man thinks you're the devil himself!" Victor told Dante with a smile on his lips. "I'll admit that it's been real good seeing the cocky bastard afraid for a change. What am I supposed to be able to do for you, though?"

"It's simple!" Dante replied. "I want to know who's all involved with both Edward and Samuel, and I need accurate locations and names."

"And if I help you, will you release my wife?"

"Let's deal with Edward and Samuel first, and then we'll discuss your wife's release," Dante told him as he stepped back and motioned for Victor to step inside his mansion.

* * *

Alinna listened and watched as both Keisha and Maxine worked Rob's body, moving from body part to body part until he was willing to give up Fish

Man's location. Alinna then saw Vanessa step up beside her on her left side, but she kept watching the twins at work.

"Alinna!"

"What 'Nessa?" Alinna answered after a moment, after feeling her sister's eyes burning into the side of her face.

"Look! I know you wanna find Fish Man. We all do! But do you really think Rob knows?"

"Vanessa, you saw Fish Man's number inside his phone."

"Yeah, I did," Vanessa interrupted. "But really, Alinna. Look at the boy. He's pissed and shit on himself at least four times. If the nigga knew anything, he would have told by now."

"So what do you say we do, Vanessa?" Alinna asked, turning to face her sister. "We came to Miami to finish this bullshit with Fish Man and—!"

"Alinna!" Maxine called out.

Alinna looked from Vanessa over to the twins and saw them both standing back away from Rob, whose head was down and his chin against his chest. Alinna walked over to the girls, with both Vanessa and Yasmine following behind her.

"What the hell happened? Wake his ass the fuck up!" Alinna ordered.

"Alinna!" Yasmine said as she stepped beside Rob. She pushed his head up by the forehead and stared into his dead eyes. "He's dead, Alinna!"

"You're joking!" Alinna said, even though she could see that Rob was seriously dead. She shook her head and cursed under her breath.

"What now, Alinna?" Keisha asked while still staring angrily at Rob's dead body.

Alinna shook her head, turned away from Rob's body, and walked out of the room. She locked eyes with Harmony as soon as she stepped out into the front room, walking upon the others waiting and smoking.

"What's up, Alinna?" Harmony asked, seeing the look on her face.

"Y'all, let's get outta here! We're leaving!" Alinna told the whole room, just as Yasmine, Vanessa, Keisha, and Maxine walked into the front room. "Yasmine, have a few of the girls get rid of the body."

"I'll help!" Keisha spoke up, nodding to Yasmine.

Alinna turned and headed for the front door with the others right behind her. She stepped outside and was met by a team of four guards, two on each side of the door. She walked away from the apartment and headed for the stairs with a guard on each side of her and two following behind. Alinna then pulled out her cell phone as she walked down the step. She was surprised that he answered after three rings.

"Who this?" Dante inquired.

"You must be busy?" she asked as she walked out to her Phantom.

"Pretty much! You good, though?"

"I'm fine. But I was—!"

"Alinna, if you good, then I'ma have to call you back, shorty. I'm in the middle of handling something right now!"

"Call me later!" Alinna told him, hanging up the phone as Yasmine was climbing inside the Phantom.

"Was that Dante?" Yasmine asked as the car door was shut.

"Yeah! I'm guessing he's most likely about to kill somebody."

"Why doesn't that surprise me?" Yasmine said, earning a smile from Alinna.

* * *

Dante kept in the shadows, sprinting up the sidewalk after hopping out of the Yukon truck as it passed the mansion. He ran straight up to the tall red brick wall that surrounded the home he was about to enter. He leaped off his right foot and grabbed the top of the wall. Dante then pulled himself up and quickly over. He remained squatted in a dark corner along the wall and began looking around the front grounds.

Dante eyed three armed guards on the same side of the wall, maybe five or ten feet apart from each other. There were also three more guards along the far wall. Dante pulled out his KA-BAR knife from its leather sleeve wrapped around his forearm. He stayed low but moved quickly and surprisingly silently as he crept up on the first guard that was less than four feet away.

"Wha!" the guard started, only for Dante to cut him off, grab him across the mouth, and slide the KA-BAR knife across his throat.

He slit his throat, killing off all sound and life.

Dante gently laid down the guard on the grass. He then shifted his eyes around the grounds again, making sure he wasn't seen before he focused on the next guard, who stood close by smoking a cigarette.

Dante took off in a sprint and made it up to the guard just as the man looked his way. Dante saw the surprised look in his eyes, just before dropping into a squat and kicking his legs out from under him with a sweep kick. He followed that up by slamming the KA-BAR knife down into the guard's chest with his left hand while covering his mouth with his right.

Once the second guard was dead, Dante looked around once again. He was just about to turn his attention to the third guard when something caught his eye from across the far side of the grounds. Dante spied a fight between Gage and one of the guards. He then heard a yell and looked at the guard closest to him take off in the direction of Gage and the other guard.

"Fuck!" Dante cursed under his breath while pulling out his Glock from its holster on his left with his right hand firing away.

Boom! Boom! Boom!

* * *

"What the!" Bruce Capri started, after jerking awake at the sound of gunfire.

However, he instantly stopped in the middle of what he was saying after finding himself staring down the barrel of a chrome gun.

"Shut the fuck up, bitch!" James said to the dark-haired, white female who lay in bed beside Capri.

James then shifted his eyes back to the drug lord once the woman balled up.

"How the hell did you get into my fucking house?" Capri asked, only for the young white male to remain silent and stare straight at him. "Did you hear me, you son of a bitch? Answer me!"

James continued to ignore the man while he lay in the bed yelling and demanding to know who he was and what was going on with all the gunfire in the mansion. James then looked at his Cartier watch and saw that they had already been inside the mansion longer than they planned on being.

"Sit the fuck down!" James demanded Capri as he watched the middle-aged drug lord climb from the bed.

"I demand to know what the hell is going on!"

"Get back in the bed!" James told him, cutting him off as he began to speak.

"You will tell me!"

Boom!

"Agghhhh!" the woman screamed after the gun went off, and Capri instantly dropped to the ground as she rushed to his side.

James stared down at the woman and Capri, who he had shot in the thigh. He shook his head wondering how someone so weak could run half of Arizona. He then thought about how Dante would have reacted if he had been in Capri's place getting shot, and James figured Dante would have killed him already.

"Having a problem in here?"

James looked over his shoulder and lost his train

of thought after hearing Dante's voice. Gage walked in behind Dante.

James looked back to Capri and said, "Naw! Just waiting on you!"

Dante walked around to stand beside James, stared down at the middle-aged man, and said, "So, this is the deadly Bruce Capri?"

"Who the hell are you people?" Capri yelled out in both anger and pain. Spit flew from his mouth as he stared hatefully up at the three men standing over him.

Dante slowly smirked while he continued to stare down at the drug boss.

He then decided to answer the man's question before killing him, and said, "I'm pretty sure Samuel Randolph already warned you about me! I'm Dante Blackwell, son-in-law to Dominic Saldana!"

"You!"

Boom! Boom! Boom! Boom!

Dante instantly ended both Bruce Capri's and the woman's lives while Bruce was in the middle of saying something. However, James completely erased the expression on his face. Dante turned and then started toward the bedroom, with both James and Gage following a few steps behind him.

* * *

Dante received calls from Dre and his team that Howard Hall was taken care of. He then got a phone call from Tony T and Wesley, and was told that Norise Booth was also taken care of; however, Wesley was hit in the left arm but was fine otherwise. Dante hung up with Tony T and called Dominic's personal number.

"Saldana!"

"It's handled!"

Dominic remained quiet for a moment after hearing what Dante just told him and was a little surprised at how fast everything was handled.

He then finally spoke up and said, "What about Edward and Samuel?"

"They're both out of the state, but should be back the day after tomorrow," Dante answered. "It'll be taken care of!"

"And Victor Elijah?"

Dante was quiet for a moment before he stated, "He has a decision to make, and it depends on what he decides is his own fate!"

"I understand fully. Keep me posted."

Dante hung up the phone with Dominic and then called Alinna. He looked out the passenger window while listening to the line ring until her voice came over the line: "You finished?"

"Not fully!" Dante answered. "Just one last thing and then we'll be done out here. What's up with you back there?"

"Well, Rob won't be a problem anymore!"

"You handed that then?" Dante asked, only to end up listening as Alinna told him about Rob dying while the twins, Keisha and Maxine, were working on him.

He hated to hear that they still had no idea where the hell Fish Man was at, and they had no way of finding out how to find the bitch nigga.

"I'll be there soon," Dante told Alinna once she finished telling him what went on in Miami. "Gimme a few days and we'll be home. I love you!"

"I love you too, Dante."

THIRTEEN

ALINNA SPENT ANOTHER FOUR days in Miami doing everything she could to find out Fish Man's location, but still turned up nothing. She allowed herself to fall back into business mode by getting more work out onto the streets and adding the heroin that she had Dante ship to her. The streets were becoming aware of the new Japanese heroin, and Alinna quickly saw the reactions to it and heard the talk that was spreading around Miami.

On the fifth day, Alinna was awoken by her ringing cell phone. She blindly reached over to the bedside table by her son, who was sound asleep beside her.

"What?" she said, eyes still closed.

"Is this Alinna Rodriguez?" the feminine voice asked.

"Who is this?"

"My name is Diamond!"

"Diamond?"

"Yes, ma'am," Diamond replied, but then said something that got Alinna's attention. "I hear you're looking for Kyle Otis, but you may know him as Fish Man!"

Wide awake now, Alinna jerked upright in bed after hearing Fish Man's name. She gripped the phone in her hand and pressed it to her ear. "Who is this?"

"Girl, I just told you. This is Diamond!"

"No! What's your real name?"

"Honey, my name is Diamond Desirous! Now do you want to know where Kyle Otis is or not?"

"How do I know this isn't some type of set up trick?"

"Child, pleeeease! Who's crazy enough to really mess with Dante Blackwell's woman!"

"All right. Where's Fish Man at?"

"Not yet, honey!" Diamond replied. "I remember hearing that there was a reward for information on Kyle Otis, and if you want this information, we need to meet so I can get paid."

"Okay! Where?" Alinna asked while listening to the time and place at which they would meet.

Alinna then hung up the phone after the conversation with the woman who had introduced herself as Diamond Desirous. She then instantly called Dante and was surprised when it went right to voice mail. She hung up and tried again.

Alinna left a message for Dante to call her back as soon as he received the message, explaining that it was gravely important. She then hung up the phone, climbed from her bed, and went to Vanessa's room to let her know about the phone call she had just received.

* * *

Dante saw the stretch Mercedes-Benz limousine as it turned inside the front guarded gate. His men were now dressed like Edward Randolph's guards who had been killed. Dante called out to James, Dre, and Gage, who all were asleep while he remained awake and staring out the bedroom window from the second-floor master.

"What's up, family?" Dre asked as he sat up from where he was stretched out across a bed.

He stared at Dante, who was still looking out the window that faced the front of the mansion.

"He's here," Dante said, before turning away from the window and leaving out the bedroom door.

Dante walked up the long hallway and was in no rush. Dre, James, and Gage were right behind him. He made it to the top of the stairs and saw Wesley, Tony T, and a team of young killers already on point. He heard the shooting start up, and seconds later the front door flew open and Edward Randolph was rushed inside the mansion by a team of four guards who were quickly gunned down.

Dante then noticed a familiar face that stood beside Edward and was staring up at him with both fear and shock. Dante slowly smiled while taking his time making his way down the stairs.

Once he got downstairs and stood a few feet away from Edward and Samuel Randolph, Dante said, "I was beginning to wonder if you were ever coming home, Edward, and then you walk through the door with gifts. How's it going, Samuel?"

"How the fuck did you get into my house?" Edward Randolph asked in a calm voice while his anger showed on his face.

"Since you asked first how I entered your house, I'll assume you know who I am already, correct?" Dante asked, but continued before Edward could attempt to say anything. "I won't make this visit any longer than it already has been. We have other business to deal with, so at this point, gentlemen, this is a good—!"

Dante peeped the move that Samuel tried to make while he was speaking. Dante pulled out his banger with his right hand from his left-side holster, just as Samuel pulled out a chrome piece from inside his suit jacket.

Boom! Boom! Boom!
Pop! Pop!

Dante watched as Samuel Randolph stumbled backward, slamming into the wall behind him. Dante felt the two slugs that skimmed into his chest, which sent him staggering backward a step. He slowly dropped to a knee while grabbing his chest, barely aware of the sounds of automatic and semiautomatic guns going off around him before he fell back onto his ass.

* * *

After letting Vanessa, Yasmine, and the other girls know about the agreed-upon meeting spot with the caller who introduced herself as Diamond, Alinna sent Yasmine to check out the location where the meeting was supposed to take place. Even though Alinna was certain that the name wasn't real, she called Greg Wilson and had him check out Diamond Desirous just to make sure.

She next called Rafael to check up on Angela's husband, Geno, to make sure that Rafael had not already murdered him.

Alinna tried Dante's phone and was not surprised to get his voicemail, since he had told her that he was planning to finish up business in Phoenix. She left a quick message and let him know the time and place of the meeting.

Alinna then showered and dressed in a navy-blue Kenneth Cole pantsuit and a pair of open-toed stiletto heels. She ate breakfast with the kids and was just finishing when Yasmine returned, with both Keisha and Maxine with her.

"What's it look like?" Alinna asked as she left the kitchen and entered the den with Yasmine and the twins following her.

"The diner is on a four-way street and sits on the corner of Main."

"Diner?" Alinna asked, a little confused.

"Royal Castle," Maxine answered.

"Wait!" Alinna said. "I thought they closed that down on 79th Street?"

"They was supposed to, but they didn't!" Keisha told Alinna. "It's still in the same spot."

Alinna nodded her head in agreement as she pictured the area she knew well.

She looked at Yasmine and said, "I want each corner blocked off, and nobody is to enter the area or the diner after we're inside."

Yasmine bowed her head slightly, and then turned and left the den.

* * *

Alinna handled some business that morning that could have waited for a later date, but it killed some time until her meeting with Diamond. She then spent some time with her sister-in-law, Melody, and went to the post office and then out to lunch. Alinna found herself liking Dante's baby sister as the two of them talked and got to know each other better, asking and answering questions.

Alinna tried Dante's number again, and by 3:30 in the afternoon she got his voicemail again. She tried calling James, Tony T, and even Wesley, but she only received their voicemails. She began to worry a bit.

By the time 5:00 p.m. rolled around, everyone began to get dressed for the meeting. Alinna then sent Rose to get Kerri for her.

"Yeah, Alinna. What's up?" Kerri asked a little while later, after entering the master bedroom and seeing Alinna dressed in a Dolce & Gabbana outfit and seated at the foot of the bed, where she was slipping on a pair of heels that matched the outfit perfectly.

"Kerri, I need you to get in contact with Dante," Alinna told her assistant. "I've got some crazy feeling that something is not right. I've called Dante's phone and even Dre, James, Wesley, and Tony T, and none of them are answering their phone. That's not like them, Kerri."

"I'll find out what's going on," Kerri told her as she pulled out her cell phone and turned to leave the bedroom, just as Yasmine and Vanessa walked in.

"You ready?" Vanessa asked, seeing that Alinna was already dressed.

"Yeah!" she answered as she walked over to her dresser and looked into the mirror.

She then picked up her back holster that held her Glock .17 that Dante had given to her. She attached it to the back of her dress pants that were part of her Dolce & Gabbana suit, and then she picked up her purse, keys, and phone. Alinna then turned and faced Yasmine and Vanessa, and caught them talking to each other in a lowered voice.

"What's with the whispering?" Alinna spoke up as she started from the bedroom door.

"We were just discussing security," Yasmine told Alinna as she and Vanessa followed her from the bedroom.

Alinna met the rest of the girls inside the den, with Harmony smiling when she walked inside. Alinna winked at her and asked if they were all ready to go.

"We're waiting on you, Gangster Mrs.!" Maxine playfully stated, earning a smile from Alinna.

Once they were all outside and saw the chauffeur standing at the back door to one of the Benz trucks, Alinna started to question about her car, only for Yasmine to beat her to it and explain, "We've decided that since your car is well-known, you wouldn't ride in it tonight for the meeting. You'll ride inside the Mercedes truck along with Vanessa and me."

Alinna looked at Vanessa, who nodded her head in agreement to what Yasmine had just explained. Alinna said nothing in response, but started toward the truck as her personal driver opened up the back door and nodded a greeting to her.

FOURTEEN

THEY ARRIVED AT THE Royal Castle fifteen minutes after leaving the mansion.

Alinna watched as all four Escalades turned off and blocked each street as both Benz trucks turned into the parking lot. She stared out her window and saw a few cars, two SUVs, and a truck parked in the lot. She then shifted her eyes toward the diner, and she could see through the windows that there was a nice-sized crowd.

"You ready?" Vanessa asked from the front seat, looking back at Alinna.

Alinna nodded her head in response to Vanessa's question. She then climbed out from the truck once the driver walked around and opened her door. She instantly spotted a team of four guards waiting for her.

Alinna then left the truck, with Vanessa and Yasmine alongside her. She walked into the middle of the four guards as one of them held open the front door to the diner for her. Yasmine walked in first, followed by Alinna, and then Vanessa bringing up the rear.

Alinna ignored the stares that she received from the other diners. She then watched as Amber, Harmony, and the twins all walked inside. Kerri then walked in talking on her cell phone with her personal bodyguard. Alinna pointed over to the far side of the diner where two tables were open. She followed Yasmine while looking around the interior of the restaurant.

"How are we supposed to find out who this chick is we're meeting?" Maxine asked as one of the guards pushed two open tables together for them.

Alinna sat down at one of the seats once the tables were pushed together.

"We're looking for a dark-skinned female wearing a pink and white jacket and a pair of pink and white Lady Air Max," she answered Maxine.

"She must be late!" Harmony announced. "I don't see nobody in here dressed like that."

Alinna looked down at her rose gold and diamond-bezeled Rolex watch. It was 6:04 p.m., the time at which they had agreed to meet. Alinna then looked to her far left on the other side of Yasmine, to where Kerri sat. She was texting on her phone, and Alinna was just about to call her assistant's name when Harmony called out to her.

"And that's who we're waiting for?" Harmony asked, nodding toward the door that was marked for employees only.

An average-height, dark brown skinned, slim and nicely-built female with done corn rolls in her hair was headed in their direction.

"Ms. Alinna Rodriguez. I'm finally meeting the baddest bitch in Miami!" Diamond said, smiling as she walked up to the table where Alinna and her girls were sitting.

However, Diamond pulled to a sudden stop as the Asian guards stepped in front of her and blocked her way.

"Who are these rice-eating muthafuckas?" Diamond inquired.

"What's your name?" Yasmine asked from her seat beside Alinna, who sat staring at the female who stood just a few feet in front of her.

"I'm supposed to be meeting with Ms. Rodriguez as we agreed. I'm Diamond Desirous."

"What type of name is Diamond Desirous?" Maxine asked.

Amber immediately spoke up and stated, "That's not his name, is it?"

"His?" Harmony and the twins all said at the same time, looking from Amber to the female.

Diamond slowly smiled at Amber and then said, "You're right! But how did you know?"

"A friend of mine is just like you, and I'm used to seeing the change. But you've had work, haven't you?" Amber asked.

Nodding her head, Diamond said, "I've almost completely finished the surgery."

"Whoa!" Maxine said, holding up her hands to stop the conversation. "I ain't the smartest bitch in the world, but is this bitch really a nigga you're talking to?"

"She's transgender," Amber corrected her, earning a smile from Diamond.

"You say you know where Fish Man is?" Alinna finally spoke up, drawing all the attention to her.

"Yes, honey! But first let's discuss the money you promised me," Diamond mentioned, folding her arms across her chest.

Alinna had Yasmine dismiss the guards, and she then looked over toward Vanessa on her right. Alinna nodded her head, which caused Vanessa to reach down and pick up the black briefcase that sat on the floor beside her right leg.

Alinna watched as Vanessa walked around the two tables to stand beside Diamond. She then laid down a briefcase on top of the table and opened it. Alinna sat watching Diamond, who slowly smiled when she stared down at the briefcase filled with money.

"Pull up a chair and sit down!" Alinna told her as Vanessa closed the briefcase back up and left it on the table.

Vanessa then returned to her seat as Diamond sat down and joined the table.

"So, you want to know where Kyle Otis got his ass at, huh?" Diamond said as she sat the briefcase on the floor on the right side of her.

Diamond was just about to continue, when Harmony cried out Alinna's name and pointed over toward the front door, with a big smile on her face.

Alinna turned around to see what Harmony was talking about and stared in surprise and happiness as she saw Dante walk into the restaurant in a knee-length, white leather coat. Dre, James, Wesley, Tony T, and Gage walked in behind him, all dressed in black with leather jackets.

"Oh, sweet Jesus! Is that the fine-ass Dante Blackwell?" Diamond asked, smiling just as wide as Harmony.

Diamond sat watching the all-too-sexy and handsome Dante walk directly up between Alinna's and the Asian woman's chairs. He then leaned down and kissed Alinna's lips and then turned his head and kissed Yasmine.

"Do I get one of those too, Mr. Sexy?" Diamond joked.

Dante barely glanced over at the woman, who was wearing almost too much pink, before he focused on Alinna and asked, "Did I miss anything?"

"Actually, we just got here!" Alinna told him, just as Gage slid over a chair for Dante to sit down.

Alinna then looked back over at Diamond, only to find her staring hungrily at Dante, and said, "Uhhh, Diamond. You can finish what you was just about to tell us about Fish Man's whereabouts."

"She knows where Fish Man is?" Dante asked, looking back at Alinna.

Diamond then spoke up and said, "Dante Blackwell, I'm sitting right here. If you have a question about me, you can definitely ask me directly, baby."

"Where's Fish Man?"

"Newark, New Jersey."

"Where at in Newark, shorty?"

"I've got that information right here," Diamond told Dante, pulling out a folded piece of pink and red paper from her pocket and handing it over to him.

Yasmine then took the paper from Diamond's hands, to which she gave her a nasty look before she focused back on Dante and said, "Kyle Otis moved to—!"

"Who the fuck is Kyle Otis?" Dre interrupted.

"Damn, Dre. You gonna let a bitch finish before you start asking questions?" Diamond asked him, giving Dre a look.

"You know Dre?" Keisha asked what everyone else was also wondering.

"Who doesn't know Dante Blackwell's brother?" Diamond began, with a matter-of-fact attitude. "Everybody knows that Dre and Dante hang together and do everything together. Shit! They act like they each other's shadow, since when you see one, you better believe the other one is lurking close by somewhere."

Dante smirked and asked, "How exactly do you know all this?"

"You're my baby daddy, and you don't even know it, Mr. Blackwell! I've loved you since I was a little girl with your fine ass!"

"Who the fuck is Kyle Otis?" Dre asked, interrupting again and earning a looking from Diamond.

"You are so disrespectful, Dre!" Diamond told him, rolling her eyes at him.

She then looked back at Dante and said, "Kyle Otis is Fish Man's real name, boo!"

"How do you know that?" Dante asked.

"You gonna be mad at me if I tell you?"

"I'ma be upset if you don't tell me!"

With a sigh, Diamond began: "Kyle and me used to be an item until he started messing with this bitch I thought was my best friend. The both of their asses left and moved away together. That's how I know where they at, because the bitch called me to talk shit about taking Kyle's lying ass."

"So Fish Man's gay, huh?" Dante asked, catching the surprised look that Diamond shot him, followed by Vanessa, Alinna, and the rest of the family.

"Fam, what the hell you talking about?" Dre asked Dante.

"Shorty," Dante started, nodding over to Diamond and then continuing, "is really a dude, but probably went through a little surgery. Am I right?"

Diamond was completely surprised that Dante recognized what she was quicker than most people could.

Diamond asked, "How is it that you recognize me, Dante?"

"Whoa! Hold up!" Tony T spoke up. "You mean to tell me that this chick is really a swinging dick?"

"Not for much longer, I ain't!" Diamond said with a smile as she looked down at the briefcase filled with the money she had received from Alinna.

Dante got back to the subject at hand and asked Diamond if she had a way to get in contact with Fish Man.

"He still calls me sometimes," she answered. "I got his number for his personal line, which is the same number on that paper that Bruce Lee's sister took out of my hand."

Diamond began explaining to Dante, only to hear Alinna ask, "You still fucking Fish Man, Diamond?"

"No! But his ass keeps asking me to come and visit him since he's been talking that he misses me and wants to see me."

"Have you been to see him?" Vanessa asked.

"No reason to!" Diamond answered. "His sorry ass made his choice. Now he's stuck with it."

"Would you consider going to visit him and helping us?" Dante asked, drawing Diamond's attention back to him.

"For you, Dante Blackwell, I'll do just about anything you ask me to!" Diamond told him, smiling across the table at him.

Dante nodded his head as two different plans began forming inside his head. He stood up from his seat, which caused the rest of the family to all stand as well. He told Kerri to get Diamond's contact information as well as her address. Dante then turned and started for the front door with both Alinna and Yasmine at his side, along with a crowded team of bodyguards.

Once they were all outside, Alinna saw Dante's Bentley Continental GT Speed that she had bought for him. She climbed in the back of the Bentley after Dante opened the car door for her. Yasmine followed behind, and then Dante got in.

James and Gage then got in the front of the car, with Gage getting behind the wheel.

As they pulled out of the lot, Alinna asked, "Why didn't you call me and let me know that you were on your way?"

"I was in the middle of handling something, and then right afterward we flew out here," Dante explained.

He then looked over toward Yasmine and inquired, "Why are you staring at me like that?"

"What's wrong with your right shoulder, Dante?" she asked him, noticing the slight stiffness in the way that he moved to his right, when all his movements were normally so smooth and strong.

Dante knew that Yasmine was very watchful of him as he simply answered, "I'm good, Yasmine!"

"What happened, Dante?" Alinna then asked, drawing his attention back to her.

Dante was not surprised that Yasmine had peeped that something was wrong.

"Have you talked with Rafael yet about Gomez?" Dante asked Alinna, changing the subject as he dug out a fresh box of Black & Milds from his pocket.

Alinna shook her head as she stared at Dante.

She then left the subject alone concerning what had happened to him, and instead answered his question, "Yes, Dante. I called Rafael, and I told him that you was on your way back and would contact him once you were home."

Dante nodded his head in response to Alinna, inhaled and then blew out the smoke from his Black & Mild, and said, "I wanna send some of the family back out to Phoenix to hold down the business while we fly out to New Jersey to deal with Fish Man!"

"What about Melody?" Alinna asked. "You do remember that she's back with us, right?"

"Yeah!" Dante answered. "That's another issue I wanna deal with. I was thinking that before we head to New Jersey, we can stop off in Syracuse to see my mother. What you think?"

"I think you should think about Natalie, Dante!" Alinna told him. "Don't you think she would want to meet your mother also?"

"She will!" he answered. "That's why she's here with me."

"Natalie's back in Miami?" Alinna asked.

"She refused to let me leave without her and Damian," Dante explained.

Alinna slowly smiled at the picture that was forming inside her head of Natalie fighting and demanding that Dante take her with him.

Alinna then looked over at Yasmine, who was quietly staring out the window, and said, "Yasmine!"

"Yes," Yasmine calmly replied, turning her head around to look at Alinna.

"How do you feel about meeting Dante's mother?"

"If Dante wishes me to meet her, then it would be an honor."

"Why wouldn't I want you to meet her?" Dante asked, interrupting the girls' conversation and staring at Yasmine.

Yasmine said nothing and then broke eye contact with Dante. She turned her head and silently began staring out the window again.

Dante watched Yasmine for a few moments before turning back to look at Alinna. He met her eyes and caught the look that she gave him before she also turned and stared silently out of her window.

Dante shook his head at what was going on, and instead dealt with the pain that was like a burning, throbbing feeling in his chest from where the Smith & Wesson .380 rounds had slammed into his right and center chest area. He was only still alive due to Natalie fighting and crying for him to wear the bulletproof vest that Nash Johnson had given him.

Dante shifted his eyes to the front of the Bentley and locked eyes with James, who was watching him through the rear-view mirror. Dante received a slight nod from James, and then he returned the nod and turned his attention back to the Black & Mild he was smoking.

FIFTEEN

ONCE THEY WERE BACK at the mansion and the family meeting that Dante had called was over, Yasmine was told by Alinna to go and check on Dante, since he left the den before anybody else could even leave their seats.

Yasmine arrived at the master bedroom and saw that the door was slightly ajar. She started to knock when Dante walked into her view. She paused once her eyes locked onto the vest that was strapped around the right area of his chest.

"You plan on standing there staring, or are you coming inside?" Dante asked her without looking back, but still catching Yasmine's reflection inside Alinna's mirror that sat on top of her dresser.

Yasmine quietly entered the bedroom and closed the door behind her. She remained standing in front of the door watching Dante as he undressed down to his black silk boxers.

"So, I guess you do want to watch?" he asked, looking back over to Yasmine.

"What happened to your chest, Dante?" she asked, staring at the vest.

"It's nothing!"

Yasmine walked over to Dante and reached up to the straps that were across his right shoulder. She gently undid them and peeled away the vest from his chest to see the dark-colored marks on the right and center areas.

"Dante, you were shot!"

"Yeah!" he replied. "But I had on a vest! This was all that was left!"

"And it hurts, doesn't it?" she asked while gently running her hand across the bruises.

Yasmine raised her eyes and met his as he stood watching her. She moved without realizing she was actually leaning in, and seconds later she was kissing him.

Dante effortlessly picked up Yasmine by the waist.

She wrapped both arms and legs around him, but before he could walk them over to the bed, she broke their kiss and breathlessly said, "No! Take us to the shower. I want to take care of your bruises, my husband."

Doing as he was asked, Dante walked into the master bathroom while still carrying Yasmine. He ignored the tightness in his chest as he gently lowered her to her feet. He then stood there as she began pushing down his boxers and telling him to step out of them.

He watched as she undressed herself. As he went to try to help her, Yasmine shook her head no. Dante stood and continued watching until she stood before him completely naked. He was surprised and completely impressed at how curvy, toned, and muscular her body was. Yet she was still softly built.

"Come, my husband!" Yasmine told him, taking his hand in hers and then turning and opening the glass shower door.

She led him into the shower and closed the shower door behind her.

Yasmine turned on the water. Once it was hot, she pulled Dante under the stream of water and saw his body tense up. She gave him a small smile. Dante said nothing nor complained, but only held his eyes locked on hers.

"This may hurt a little bit!" she told him, after picking up the soap and getting her hands nice and soapy.

Yasmine then began massaging the muscles on Dante's chest, and she could hear the grunting sounds he made when she added a little pressure. After a while, she felt him begin to relax. When his face relaxed as well, Yasmine smiled at him and asked, "How does that feel, my husband?"

"Better!" he answered, pulling her up against him.

Dante kissed her and felt her arms wrap around his neck as she lay into him. He picked her up again, and she once again wrapped her legs around him. She moaned once Dante turned her against the wall on her side. She felt his hardness press against her womanhood. Yasmine felt his hand slide in between their bodies and then felt his manhood position at the opening of her wetness. She broke the kiss and fully leaned back against the wall while staring Dante directly in his eyes. He began pushing himself inside of her, but suddenly stopped after barely getting the head inside.

"Yasmine!" Dante said, staring hard at her after what just had happened. "Why didn't you tell me?"

Yasmine softly spoke, "It was meant for me to only give myself to my husband, Dante! I've never been with any man ever until now. I understand you know nothing of the customs of my people, but for us to do this completes our bond and our marriage to each other. This is something I want, Dante. Do you want this as well?"

Yasmine held his eyes for what almost seemed too long. She then felt him begin pushing forward inside of her again. She closed her eyes and hissed a little once he broke through her hymen. Dante was surprised at how full she felt between her legs as he pushed more and more into her until he was completely inside. She held onto his neck as he held still a few moments, which allowed her to get used to the size of him inside of her.

"You all right?" he softly asked, speaking into her ear.

Nodding her head, Yasmine opened her eyes and leaned back to meet his. She slowly smiled and kissed Dante's lips as she felt him begin to move in and out of her.

"Dante! Yesssss! It feels so good, my husband!"

Dante gripped her waist and pressed her back against the wall as he slowly pushed in and out of her vice-like gripping pussy. He tried to focus on not cumming too soon while making love to Yasmine, who was now speaking softly into his ear in Japanese as his face lay against the side of her neck.

Dante worked hard getting Yasmine through her first orgasm. She screamed his name and squirted as he exploded seconds behind her from the way her pussy squeezed and milked his dick. He poured his seed deep inside her.

* * *

After three orgasms, Dante found out that Yasmine was multi-orgasmic, cumming a total of six times back-to-back. He left her asleep in the bed, dressed in gray sweatpants, and headed out the bedroom door to find Alinna and Natalie up and watching a movie together in the den.

"You're still alive? I'm surprised!" Alinna said jokingly, after noticing that he was standing in the doorway watching the two of them.

Dante entered the den and walked over to the sofa as both girls moved apart and pulled him down between them. He took the bowl of popcorn from Natalie's lap and began eating.

"You hungry, baby?" Natalie said with a smile as she watched him.

"Why do I feel like you two set me up?" Dante asked while stuffing his mouth full of popcorn. "You both talked to Yasmine and sent her to find me, didn't you?"

"Actually, I sent her to find you!" Alinna told him. "I spoke with her, and then I spoke with Natalie so there wouldn't be any misunderstanding. But, yes, you were set up since Yasmine admitted that she was a virgin. And there's one thing I know about Asian women, Dante. It's proven that they are very sexual women and love to have sex with their man."

"They're like vampires!" Dante replied while still stuffing his mouth.

Both Alinna and Natalie laughed at him.

Dante then changed the subject for a moment and said, "I was thinking about this shit with Fish Man, and I wanna use Diamond, but I think we're gonna need someone else with Diamond since Fish Man's messing with Diamond's friend."

"So what are we going to do then?" Alinna asked him. "I'm pretty sure none of the girls know any transgenders other than Amber, and I don't think—!"

"I know someone!" Natalie spoke up, drawing the attention to her from both Dante and Alinna.

"You know somebody, Natalie?" Alinna asked her.

"My friend Mari, back in Phoenix, who you all met who owns that restaurant. She has a brother who's been through the whole transformation with his sex change to a her. His name is now Meline Elysse."

"Would Fish Man like her, though?" Alinna asked Natalie.

Natalie sat forward and picked up her cell phone from the glass coffee table.

As she scrolled through her pictures, she said, "This is her here!"

Alinna took the phone from Natalie and looked at the picture, and was completely in shock at how beautiful Mari's brother/sister was.

"Dante, look!"

"Yeah!" Dante replied, barely glancing at the phone before looking toward Natalie and asking, "You think he'd help us?"

"Y'all have to talk to him, but it's best if you ask Mari to ask him, since he's crazy about her and does everything for her," Natalie explained as she took back her phone from Alinna. "Do you want me to call her?"

Dante slowly nodded his head and then allowed his thoughts to flow through his mind a moment before he said, "Yeah! Go ahead and call, but tell both Mari and Meline that I've got $25,000 each for the both of them for their help!"

Dante looked back at Alinna as Natalie made the call to Mari, and said, "I know this is your beef, but you know how I feel about shit that involves you. But I'm going to fall back and let you take the lead.

Whatever you want done is on your call. I'm at your call, shorty!"

Alinna smiled at Dante and leaned toward him. She laid her right hand against the side of his face as she passionately kissed his lips. Just as she was really getting into her kiss with him, Natalie cleared her throat and then called out Dante's name.

Dante winked and smirked at Alinna and then smiled at her.

He then turned his attention back to Natalie and said, "What's up, beautiful?"

SIXTEEN

DANTE GOT EVERYONE ON the same page once Mari and Meline were flown out to Miami and Diamond was brought to the mansion. Dante let it be known that Alinna was taking the lead in dealing with the issue concerning Fish Man. But he also made sure that all the men understood that whatever any of the women needed, they would give to them without question.

Once the plan was set and discussed among the family, and it was explained that the family would first stop in Syracuse with Dante's sister, Melody, so Dante could meet his mother, Alinna told everyone to get ready to leave in a few hours.

"Yo, Dante!" James called out, catching him as he, Yasmine, Natalie, and Alinna were walking off and heading to the bedroom.

"What's up, family?" Dante asked as he turned back to see what James wanted.

James cut his eyes over toward Alinna, Yasmine, and Natalie, and he caught the smile that Alinna gave him before she turned and led the other two women away.

James looked back to a smirking Dante and said, "Bruh, what's up? Why didn't you tell me you were bringing Mari out here?"

"Let me guess, playboy, you tripping because Maxine's about to wild out because Mari's not about to play the side chick, right?" Dante asked with a smirk. "My advice, J! Start with Maxine first, playboy, because shorty showed that she can play the insane game already!"

James just shook his head as he watched Dante walk off.

He then felt arms wrap around him from behind.

Maxine kissed him on the neck and then whispered, "We still got some time before we leave. Let's go back to your room and play around a little."

James sighed as he gently pulled her arms loose from around him.

He turned to face her and was just opening his mouth to say something, when he heard, "Hey, baby! Can I talk to you a minute, James?"

"Hey, baby!" Maxine repeated with an instant attitude as she turned to look next to James at the Spanish female who was supposed to be Natalie's friend.

Maxine then looked back at James and said, "What the hell this bitch needs to talk to you about, James?"

"Shit!" James said, shaking his head.

He looked back at Mari and saw the confused look on her face as she stood staring back and forth from him to Maxine. He could already see shit about to blow up in his face.

* * *

Alinna waited outside next to the Bentley and talked with Dre, Tony T, and Wesley. The others began pouring out of the front door of the mansion all ready to leave and head out to the G4 that she had rented, which Alinna thought about buying.

Dante turned back to continue talking with his brothers, when he heard yelling and cursing. He swung his attention back to the front door and saw James walking outside, with both Mari and Maxine following behind him.

Dante slowly smirked when he saw what was going on with his boy James as both women were yelling at him.

Dante then spoke up to give his boy a break, "Max! Mari! Give it a break for a minute! Let the man handle his business!"

Maxine sucked her teeth and shot James a look before she rolled her eyes and stomped off.

"We will talk James! Dante can't save you every time!" Mari told him before she also stormed off.

James could only shake his head as he watched Mari walk off.

He then looked over at Dante, only for Tony T to playfully ask, "Damn, J! When you decide to become a player, playboy? You got a fine-as-hell deranged lunatic and a sexy Spanish chick after you. You may need your own bodyguard, don't ya think?"

"Real funny, T!" James said, unable to help smiling while the others laughed.

"You'll be all right, family!" Dante told James as Alinna, Yasmine, and Natalie exited the front door, followed by the guards carrying their suitcases.

"Are we ready?" Alinna asked as she walked up to Dante.

"We're waiting, y'all!" Dre answered, but then asked, "Y'all got enough bags, though?"

"Mind your business, nigga!" Alinna told Dre playfully, before looking back at Dante and saying, "I'm letting Natalie, Mari, and Meline use the Phantom. Natalie is going to have Rose and Emmy with her to watch the kids when we're in Syracuse visiting your mother."

"Where's Melody?" Dante asked.

"She's coming!" Alinna answered as she and Yasmine walked over to the backseat door of the Bentley.

The women stopped as they watched a cocaine-white BMW M4 pull inside the front gate of the mansion. They stood where they were as Dante, James, and Gage stepped out in front of the Bentley followed by Dre, Tony T, and the rest of the crew.

"Dante, relax!" Vanessa called out, pushing through the crowd to stand between him and Dre. "That's Kyree. The twins' brother."

"Where the hell he been at?" Dante asked as the M4 came to a stop a few feet in front of him and the others.

"I had him out in Atlanta handling some business for the family," Vanessa explained. "That's why he didn't fly out to Phoenix with the rest of us when you called."

"What's up, everybody?" Kyree said as he and two of his boys walked up to stop in front of Dante, Vanessa, and the rest of the family. "What's going on, Dante, man?"

"You tell me!" Dante replied as he stared Kyree directly into his eyes. "You handled business out there in Atlanta?"

"No doubt, boss man! I made sure six different spots were set up all over Atlanta, and I even brought back some information on some new buyers who want to fuck with the family," Kyree explained, holding up his cell phone to Dante, who simply nodded his head.

"Good work, youngin'! Get with Vanessa, and she'll fill you in on what's going on."

Dante turned away and walked back over to the Bentley as the others began making their way to the other vehicles that were waiting. He then climbed into the car with both Alinna and Yasmine and shut the back door.

"Everything okay?" Alinna asked.

"Everything's good, shorty!"

* * *

Once they were all out on the airstrip where both the rented G4 and Dominic's G4 were waiting, Dante had Wesley and Amber explain to the team that he wanted them to fly back to Phoenix and hold down business until they got word from either him or Alinna. Wesley was still somewhat out of commission after taking two shots back in Phoenix. Dante then had the rest of the family and crew load up onto the rented G4.

"Dante!" Melody called out to her brother once everyone was on the G4 flying to Syracuse.

She waved Dante over to where she and the twins were sitting and talking.

"What's up, baby girl?" Dante said, sitting down beside her, only to have Mya rush over to him and climb into his lap.

As he smiled at her, Melody looked back at Dante and explained, "I just hung up with Momma. I told her we was flying to see her. She's excited, Dante!"

"Daddy! Are we gonna see Grandmomma?" Mya asked, looking up at Dante.

"Yeah, baby girl!" Dante answered as he began wondering how things would play out once he was face-to-face with his birth mother.

* * *

Dante slept most of the flight from Miami to Syracuse, but he was awoken as the jet was landing on the airstrip in Syracuse. He was surprised at how suddenly nervous he was as he stepped off the jet along with everyone else. He followed his sister, Natalie, and Alinna over to the stretch Escalade limo while the others climbed into the four other Cadillac Escalades that Alinna had arranged to be waiting for them.

Once Yasmine finished dealing with security and was inside the Escalade limo with Vanessa, Dre, Tony T, Harmony, and the others, Dante told the driver that they were ready. Melody gave the chauffeur the address where they were going, and he drove off.

"So, how long are we going to be here, Dante?" Diamond asked him from where she sat next to Mari's brother/sister Meline.

"Not long!" Dante answered, shifting his eyes over to his sister when he heard that she was talking to their mother on the phone.

* * *

Brenda hung up from the call. She was both excited and nervous as she began pacing back and forth in the front room of their four-bedroom, two-and-a-half-bath house in which she lived with her husband and daughter.

"Baby, you all right?" Dwayne asked, after walking into the room and seeing his wife pacing the floor.

"Melody just called, Dwayne!" Brenda told her husband. "They're home and should be at the house in twenty minutes."

Dwayne smiled at his normally calm and in-control wife as he walked over to her and grabbed her in his arms. He kissed her passionately on the lips for a few minutes, feeling her body instantly relax against his. He slowly pulled back out of the kiss and watched her eyes slowly open to meet his.

"Feel better?" he asked.

She slowly smiled, nodded her head, and said, "Yes!"

Brenda then leaned in for another kiss when the doorbell rang, causing her to pause and her eyes to grow wide.

"Relax, Brenda!" Dwayne told her as he released his wife and walked over to the front door.

He unlocked it and then opened the door to find Brenda's older sister, Gina, and her husband standing there, along with their son coming up the walkway.

"Where's my nephew?" Gina cried, pushing past her brother-in-law to see her sister standing in the middle of the floor. "Brenda, where he at? Where's my nephew at?"

"What? How you even know?" Brenda started, but then said, "Melody called and told you that Dante was coming, didn't she?"

"She called me yesterday!" Gina confessed as both her son and husband walked into the front room with Dwayne. "Where is he?"

"He's not here yet, Gina," Brenda told her sister while hugging her brother-in-law and then her nephew. "Where's Lisa? Why isn't she here?"

"She's out with her boyfriend," Gina's son, Floyd Jr., answered. "She claims she's coming over later."

"So, how long are they—!" Gina started, but stopped when the house phone rang.

Brenda looked over at the phone on the coffee table, picked up the cordless phone, and answered, "Hello."

"Mama, we're coming down the street now!" Melody told her mother as soon as she heard her mother's voice on the line.

Brenda dropped the phone after hearing what her daughter had to say and took off for the door. She snatched it open and stepped out onto the porch, just as a pearl-white Escalade stretch limousine and four black Cadillac Escalades pulled up in front of the house. Brenda didn't even notice that the rest of her family had stepped out onto the porch as well.

She stared as the back door to the limo opened and saw a young, white man step out, followed by a dark-skinned man who looked just as young as the white man.

"Who are they?" Gina asked, also watching the white and black men look around until an Asian woman stepped out of the limousine.

At least thirty Asian men dressed in suits climbed out of the four SUVs that had parked in front of the limo and behind it.

Brenda saw Melody hop out from the limo with a big smile on her face. Brenda felt her heart beat harder and faster against her ribs as she watched Melody reach back inside the limo and begin to pull someone out.

"Oh my God!" Gina cried in disbelief as Melody wrapped her arms around the same Dante Blackwell that was all over the world news and known almost worldwide. "Brenda, he's gorgeous. He's even more handsome in person, girl!"

Brenda's hands covered her mouth as Melody walked her son up the walkway and up to the porch. Brenda wasn't even aware that she was crying as she stared into the eyes of her son.

"Mama, here's Dante!" Melody introduced while smiling at her mother.

"Oh my God!" Brenda cried, rushing over to her son and throwing her arms around his neck.

She hugged him tightly and felt his arms wrapping tightly around her. She completely broke down crying even harder from sheer happiness.

* * *

Dante first met his mother's sister and brother-in-law as well as his cousin, Floyd. Brenda then introduced him to her husband, Dwayne Bell. In turn, Dante then introduced Alinna, Natalie, and Yasmine, followed by Dre, Vanessa, and the other Blackwell family members.

"So you're my daughter-in-law?" Brenda asked, seeing a huge diamond ring on Alinna's finger.

"Yes, ma'am," she replied, but then respectfully said, "But, ma'am, you also have two other daughters-in-law."

"Excuse me?" Brenda and Gina said in unison, looking from Alinna to Dante, who was talking with Floyd and Dwayne.

Brenda looked back at Alinna and said, "Alinna, I don't understand what you're saying, sweetheart. How can Dante have more than one wife?"

"It's a long story!" Alinna admitted, smiling at her mother-in-law.

"I want to hear this!" Gina said as she pulled Alinna by the hand, leading her over to the sofa and sitting her down beside her. "All right! We're listening, Alinna! Talk!"

SEVENTEEN

DANTE LEFT THE HOUSE with his mother as they walked the neighborhood and just talked and got to know one another. James and Gage followed in one of the Escalades. Dante listened as his mother explained about his childhood and the problems she had with his father. She also explained how she had lost him after his father took him away, and how she was unable to find him while she was pregnant with Melody.

Dante then explained how his father and his father's best friend raised him, and how his father's friend took him in when his father died. He also admitted that he mostly stayed with Dre and Dre's mother.

"So how did you meet Alinna?" Brenda asked him, smiling up at Dante as she held her arm around his waist and leaned against him while they continued walking.

Dante didn't want to lie to his mother, so he admitted the whole truth to her. To his surprise, she took it all so calmly and with a smile.

"She's good for you, Dante!" Brenda told him once he finished explaining. "I really like her, and she even explained to me about Yasmine and Natalie, and I have some beautiful grandbabies."

"Thanks!"

"But, there's one thing I want to ask you, Dante."

"I'm listening."

"I know what you do for a living. I'm sure half the world knows what you do for a living. Dante Blackwell is a known name. But hearing all you've gained so far, don't you think it's about time you left the streets alone or at least stopped being active on the streets unless you have to be active? I'm not telling you what you're doing is wrong, because what you don't know is that I was once out in the streets doing the same thing Alinna is doing now. The only difference is that I didn't have a Dante Blackwell to look out for me. So, basically what I'm saying is you've taken over most if not all of Miami and the streets know and definitely fear and respect you. So why not disappear into the background, Dante? You should know that no one stays on top forever. You've built an empire for your family; now live like the king I know you are, my son. Show your daughter a good life, and teach your sons to be men—men of power—and what is to be expected from them. You understand what I'm saying, sweetheart?"

Dante slowly nodded his head yes and then said, "I understand. But there are just two last things I have to take care of before I step back."

He then explained about Fish Man and New Jersey, his promise to Monica, and the problems with Angela.

Dante was surprised when his mother said, "Talk to your cousin Floyd. He hangs out over in New Jersey selling weed. He may know something about this Fish Man person you're looking for."

Dante nodded his head after hearing his mother's advice. He then wrapped his right arm around her shoulders as she leaned more into him and then continued their walk.

* * *

Once back at the house, Dante noticed a Lincoln Navigator that was now parked in front of the house. He made contact with James as he was climbing from the Escalade, and nodded toward the Navigator and then the house.

"Whose Navigator, Mama?" Dante asked, pulling his mother to a gentle stop as James went to check it out while Gage went ahead to check the house.

Brenda smiled when she caught the silent instructions her son had given to his men, who responded instantly with no question.

Brenda then looked at Dante and said, "Honey, it's just probably your cousin Lisa and her boyfriend, Eddie."

Dante nodded his head in response to his mother's answer. He then caught the nod that James gave him that everything was okay.

Dante then led his mother up to the front door and heard Gage whisper to him in passing, "It's a cousin and her boyfriend."

"I told you!" Brenda told Dante, smiling as she released him and then stepped inside the house.

Dante slowly smirked, realizing how on point his mother was. He then followed her into the house and paused as he caught some movement on his right side, only to see James swiftly move and grab the light-skinned man within seconds. The young man was on his knees with his arm folded behind his back, crying out in pain.

"Dante!" Alinna and Natalie cried out.

Dante stared down at the guy who James held down. He heard his mother call his name with a demanding tone. Dante then called out to James, who quickly released the man.

"Who's this?" Dante asked, looking over at Alinna, who shook her head and had a smile on her face.

"He's my boyfriend!"

Dante turned his head around and looked at the brown-skinned female who had just spoken up. She stared at him with a smile on her face.

"You must be Lisa, right?" Dante asked.

"Everybody calls me LaLa though!" she told him as she slowly looked him over. "And you are fine as hell! You sure we family, nigga?"

Laughing at Lisa's question, Dante shook his head, looked at her boyfriend, and said, "You good, playboy?"

"Yeah!" Eddie answered, rubbing his shoulder while cutting his eyes over toward James.

He looked back to Dante and said, "You're famous, man! Everybody in Syracuse is talking about Dante and Alinna Blackwell. You got mutha—!"

"Eddie!" Brenda interrupted, giving the young man a hard look.

"Sorry, Mrs. Bell!" Eddie apologized.

Dante smirked as he shook his head again. He looked around for Floyd Jr. and noticed that all the guys were gone.

"Where's everybody at?"

"Mr. Bell and the other others out back, Dante," Natalie told him. "They're barbecuing."

"Baby, why don't you go on out back with the others," Brenda told her son with a smile. "And try to relax."

Dante smiled at his mother and kissed her cheek as he walked past her. Every woman in the house stared at him as he walked toward the screen door to the backyard.

* * *

Dante saw Floyd Jr. standing with Dre, Dwayne, Tony T, Floyd Sr., and a few of the crew members. Dante noticed that Kyree was standing off to the side a few feet talking on his cell phone, nodding to the young hustler after catching his eye.

"Floyd, let me holla at you real quick, youngin'!" Dante told his cousin.

He then nodded to Dwayne to let him know he would be right back.

Dante stepped away from the others a few feet and got straight to the point: "My mom told me you hustle out in New Jersey. That true? You know a guy named Fish Man?"

"I know the name, and I've heard about the dude, but I've never met him. I've seen the dude a few times out at this club in Brooklyn. He's known for going there almost every Saturday, but why don't you get at that nigga Eddie? He fucks with them Jersey niggas, fam!"

"Do me a favor! Go get that nigga for me!"

Dante watched as Floyd walked back inside the house, and Dre and Tony T walked up beside him.

"What the play, bruh?" Tony T asked as he stood on Dante's right while Dre was on his left.

"Supposedly, this dude Eddie deals with Fish Man over in Newark," Dante explained.

"Here comes the nigga now, fam!" Dre announced, nodding to the back door as Floyd Jr. and Eddie stepped out of the house and headed in their direction.

"What's up, Dante?" Eddie said as he and Floyd walked up, stopping in front of Dante and his boys. "You wanna get at me?"

"I hear you fuck with some niggas over in Newark. That true?" Dante asked the boy, staring directly into his eyes.

"Yeah!" Eddie replied. But after seeing the look on Dante's and his boys' faces, he asked, "What's good?"

"You know a nigga named Fish Man?" Tony T asked him.

"Who doesn't?" Eddie answered. "Dude's supposedly from y'all's way, but moved up here a few months ago and blew up with the coke game. Word is he's fucking with some Cuban dude that's got the nigga Fish Man flooding the streets."

"Flooding the streets, huh?" Dante repeated with a smirk on his face.

Dante looked over to Floyd who was texting and said, "Uh, yo, cuzo!"

Floyd looked up from his phone at Dante and answered, "What's up, fam?"

"You in the streets, right?"

"I'm doing a little something. Why?"

"How would you like to step your game up to some boss shit?" Dante asked him. "We family, so since you out here I'ma front you whatever you want: weed, heroin, coke, whatever! You interested?"

"What? Hell yeah!" Floyd cried out, hyped up at what he was hearing.

"All right! This is what we gonna do!" Dante began. "I'ma deal with this Fish Man, but now I'm seeing a different plan. We about to take over Newark and put New York in a headlock. We gonna end up chilling out here a lot longer than we actually planned. But I'ma get you set up out here before we leave. Can you handle what I'm about to bless you with?"

"No doubt, fam!"

Dante nodded his head and said, "All right. Get your team together and bring 'em by my hotel. But don't bring nobody you can't trust with your life. If I feel the muthafucka is fake, I'ma body him myself, so be sure who you bring to see me!"

"I'm all over it, fam!" Floyd said, dapping up with Dante.

"Yo, Dante!" Eddie called out. "I know we not family, but I'm trying to get with the team. Put the boy on, done!"

Dante stared at Eddie for a few moments, and then shifted his eyes over to Floyd and said, "It's your call, cuzo. You know dude better than I do, but understand you're responsible for homeboy if you bring him on. What's your decision?"

Floyd looked at Eddie a few minutes, and considering that what Dante had just told him was actually a warning, he slowly nodded his head, looked back toward Dante, and said, "Yeah, I'll fuck with him, fam!"

EIGHTEEN

DANTE LEFT HIS MOTHER'S house a little after 11:00 p.m., kissing her goodbye but promising to stop by in the morning for breakfast. He then hugged his Auntie Gina and Uncle Floyd, and dealt with a clinging Lisa who wanted to be walked out to Eddie's Navigator, only to make him promise to go out with her before leaving to return to Miami.

"You staying with Mama or you coming with us?" Dante asked Melody once he walked back over to stand with the others beside the limo.

"I'ma stay with Mama and Dwayne tonight," she answered, smiling as she stepped into Dante and hugged him. "I'll see you in the morning, right?"

Nodding his head and smiling, Dante turned to Dwayne, shook his hand, and said, "You're all right, Dwayne! My mom looks happy, and as long as she stays that way, we'll be cool!"

"Dante!" Brenda said, giving him a look and placing her hands on her hips.

"What I say?" Dante asked, raising both his hands up in surrender, only to cause his mother to break down a smile before hugging him again.

"It was good meeting you three," Brenda said, pulling away from Dante and turning to face Alinna, Yasmine, and Natalie.

Dante turned to Floyd Jr. while his mother said her goodbyes to the girls. He then said a few quick words to Floyd, who nodded his head in understanding.

Once inside the Escalade limo, the car barely moved more than five feet when Alinna spoke up, "What are you planning, Dante?"

Looking from his window to Alinna, Dante simply said, "There's a change of plans!"

"What type of change?"

Dante began to explain to the whole family, since they were already inside the limo and staring at him and waiting for an answer. He began by breaking down the conversation he had with Floyd Jr. earlier, and he then further explained the benefits of his plan.

"So let me understand something," Alinna began as soon as Dante finished talking. "So you're not only interested in getting rid of Fish Man, but now you want to take over not only New Jersey but New York as well, Dante?"

"Pretty much!" he answered, but then said, "I was thinking that since Amber and Wesley are already in Phoenix holding things down, Harmony and Tony T can head back to Miami and hold things down there. Dre and Vanessa can control New Jersey, and we'll maintain control out here in New York."

"And how long is this supposed to go on for?" Alinna asked him.

"Once Fish Man is dealt with, both Vanessa and Dre can get settled in Jersey, and Harmony and Tony T can fly back home. And just until shit gets settled out her, everybody can stay where they're at."

"How long, Dante?"

"A few months."

Alinna stared at her husband and understood Dante's real reason for wanting to remain in Syracuse.

She shook her head as she looked around at the others, and said, "What do you guys think? How do you all feel about this?"

"I'm with whatever my brother says!" Dre answered.

"Wherever my man is, is where I'ma be at!" Vanessa replied.

"We're with it too!" Tony T spoke up, looking over at Harmony, who shook her head in agreement.

"Yasmine! Natalie! What do you all think?" Alinna asked them.

"I go where Dante goes!" Yasmine replied, staring directly at her husband.

"I don't mind. But I would want to fly home to see my parents and let Damian see his grandparents," Natalie explained.

Alinna nodded her head and then looked at Dante and said, "There's no need to ask James and Gage since the two of them won't leave your side anyway. So I guess we have work to do."

Dante slowly smirked at Alinna, and then he began breaking down what little of the plan he had put together so far inside his head.

* * *

Dante reached the hotel at which Alinna had rented out the entire top two floors for the family and security. Dante then led Alinna, Natalie, Yasmine, Rose, and Emmy up to the penthouse suite. They would all be staying together until they decided to either buy or rent a house.

Dante handed a sleeping Mya off to Emmy and watched and she and Rose led the kids off to the back room. He then turned and walked over to the sliding glass door that led out onto a terrace while the three women were changing.

"What time is Floyd and them supposed to get here?" Alinna asked, after closing the glass door and then stepping up next to Dante, who was leaning against the metal rail.

Dante lifted up his wrist and checked the time on his Mickey Mouse, diamond-bezeled Cartier watch.

"They should be here in twenty minutes," he answered.

Alinna leaned against Dante, only to have him wrap his arm around her.

She hugged his waist and after a silent moment said, "Are you sure about this whole thing with your cousin Floyd, Dante?"

Dante nodded his head, even though Alinna wasn't paying attention.

"There's something about him. I think my mom sent me to him for this reason," Dante replied.

"Brenda sent you at Floyd?"

"Yeah!" Dante answered. He then explained how his mother suggested he speak with Floyd, since he was already on the streets.

"So this Cuban guy that's backing Fish Man. What are we going to do if we have to war with him about Fish Man?"

"I've already been thinking about that," Dante admitted. "I'ma ask Floyd about this guy. I want a name, and then I'ma see if Monica and Nash Johnson—!"

"Dante!" Yasmine interrupted as she slid open the door. "The front desk just called up to let you know that Floyd Brown is here. I told them to let him up."

Dante nodded his head in response and took another pull on his Black. He then put out his cigar, blew out the smoke, and then pushed off the rail. He released Alinna as he turned and walked back into the room, with Alinna following him.

Once the knock sounded on the front door, Yasmine went to answer it, letting the two guards stationed there know that Floyd and his four friends were okay to visit. She then stepped back to allow Floyd and company to enter.

"What's good, fam?" Floyd said, dapping up with Dante as he stood beside Alinna, who sat inside a tall back-cushioned chair with her legs crossed.

He nodded to her and received a nod in return.

Floyd began by making introductions with the only girl in the group, "Fam, this is my shorty, Nicole, but everybody calls her Nina. The black-as-hell stocky one is Beast, and the twins are Kaos and Corrupt."

"Kaos and Corrupt, huh?" Dante repeated with a smile as he looked from one light-brown skinned man to the other.

Dante then nodded to Floyd, who stepped back within his team.

"I'm pretty sure my cousin explained to each of you what you all are here for tonight. And seeing as the four of you still came with Floyd answers if any of you want to become a part of what's about to happen. Correct?" Dante said.

"No doubt, boss man!" Beast answered. "Who doesn't wanna fuck with the realist gangster walking and breathing?"

Dante nodded to the big man, and then introduced Alinna and Yasmine to the group.

"Each of you knows who I am, but you all have to understand that I'm not the sole power behind this family. Meet my wife and the other half of the Blackwell family: Alinna Blackwell."

After hearing whispers coming mostly from Nina and Beast, Dante continued, "And behind you is my third wife, Yasmine Kim! These two are among six others who are part of this family. You all will meet them at a later time."

"You said the Asian chick is your third wife?" Nina interrupted. "How many wives do you even have? I mean, you fine as hell and all, but damn, nigga!"

Dante chose to ignore Nina's comments, looked over at Alinna, and then said, "They're all yours!"

* * *

Dante spent the next two-and-a-half hours listening to Alinna break down important things to Floyd and his crew, and she even explained exactly how the family handled their business. Dante answered a few questions concerning wars that were possibly going to happen once they began their takeover through New Jersey and New York. Finally, Yasmine even added a few words concerning security and wars that they were facing. Dante ended the discussion with a few more things concerning areas that were the strongest and weakest.

He then directed his next question to Floyd: "Floyd, tell me something. Who's the Cuban who's backing Fish Man?"

"I just hear it's some Cuban named Garcia," Floyd answered. "But then I just remembered something, fam! If you're really trying to find out some real information about both Fish Man and that Garcia dude, I know somebody who can help you out."

"I'm listening!" Dante said.

"I ain't sure how you're gonna feel about this dude, but he's known for working for the money."

"Floyd!" Alinna spoke up. "Dante doesn't like repeating himself, so it's best to just say what you're gonna say!"

Floyd looked back at his cousin and saw the seriousness in his eyes. "Dude's with the NYPD. His name is Aaron Howard, and he's a lieutenant detective," Floyd said.

"Yasmine!" Dante called, seeing his wife quickly step forward. "Tell Kerri that I want her to find out whatever she can on a Lieutenant Aaron Howard."

Dante received a slight bow in reply from Yasmine.

He then focused back on Floyd and his crew and stated, "If there are no more questions, then remember what was said here and be ready for work when the time comes."

* * *

After Floyd and his crew left the hotel, Dante took a trip to the suite where Diamond, Meline, and Mari were staying, to discuss his plans.

"Hey, sexy!" Diamond said, smiling after answering the door and seeing Dante.

She stepped back and allowed her dream husband to enter the suite.

"Where's Meline and Mari?" Dante asked as he walked further into the room and looked around.

"Mari's with her man!" Diamond answered, walking past Dante in a pair of tight-ass-hugging booty shorts and a man's wifebeater that was cut in half to show her stomach and belly ring.

"And Meline?" he asked as he leaned back against the dresser beside the television, watching Diamond try to put on a show.

"You come to see me or her?" Diamond asked with an attitude, placing her hands on her hips.

"I came to discuss business!" Dante replied, ignoring Diamond's attitude, only to hear a door open up.

Dante shifted his eyes to the hallway to see Mari's light-skinned brother/sister walk in wearing Hello Kitty booty shorts and a white-and-pink matching top that was too small for the D cup implants she had.

"Hey, papi! What are you doing here?" Meline cried out happily as she rushed over to kiss Dante's cheek.

"I wanna talk to both you and Diamond," Dante told her while catching and ignoring the look that Diamond was giving him.

"So, what's up, papi?" Meline asked, sitting down on the sofa and folding her feet under her as Diamond walked past, noticing her attitude.

"All right! I want you to listen up clearly, because starting early tomorrow morning, you two are going to start things off with Fish Man," Dante began, looking from Meline to Diamond. "Diamond, when you call Fish Man and let him know that you're here in New Jersey, I also want you to introduce him to Meline. Make him think that you two are best friends."

"His ho-ish ass probably just gonna try to fuck her too!" Diamond stated angrily.

"That's the plan!" Dante stated. "I want you both to seduce him, but not too fast or too soon. Make him choose the two of you first, but I want you two to also try and get as much information out of him as you can about where his spots are located and where he's getting his work from."

"And who's going to protect us if something happens, Dante?" Diamond asked him.

"Don't worry! You'll have someone close by if you need him; and if you just want to contact me, you'll have a number to reach me at. But only use it if it's an emergency!"

"Damn!" Diamond cried. "Why'd you look at me like that when you said that, Dante?"

Dante ignored Diamond's question and began to say something else, when the front door swung open and a screaming Mari was carried into the suite in James's arms. Dante sat looking over the whole scene and noticed that Mari's clothes were ripped and her lip was bleeding.

"Allow James to deal with his woman!" Dante said as he pushed off the dresser once James had Mari locked inside the back bedroom.

Dante then left the suite, with both Diamond and Meline seated on the sofa.

* * *

Dante arrived back at his own suite and was not surprised when he barely walked through the door and could hear Maxine yelling. He then saw her and Keisha, Alinna, Vanessa, Harmony, and Yasmine all in the front room.

"Dante!" Maxine yelled as soon as she laid eyes on him.

Dante shut the door, only to have it pushed back open by Kerri, who rushed past carrying a clear plastic bag of ice. Dante shut the door again and then started toward his bedroom, only for Maxine to cut him off.

"Dante, you either gonna do something, or I swear I'ma kill that bitch about my man!" Maxine spit out at Dante.

"What exactly do you expect me to do, Maxine?" Dante asked her. "This is between you, James, and Mari. You three gotta handle that."

"Naw. That bitch is about to get bodied!" Keisha said from across the room.

"I'ma say this once!" Dante said, looking from Keisha back to Maxine. "Nobody is to step to Mari unless it's a fight between Maxine and Mari. If anybody pulls any kind of weapon out on Mari or if she's jumped, then I promise I'll get involved! Are we clear?"

"Oh, so you taking that bitch's side?" Keisha asked nastily.

"It's not about taking sides, Keisha!" Dante told her as he looked back at Maxine and then more calmly said, "The both of you are a part of this family, Maxine. I can't get in between what's going on with you, James, and Mari. You three gotta handle that!"

Dante then kissed Maxine's forehead and turned and entered his bedroom to change his clothes. He needed to get his own mind right.

NINETEEN

DIAMOND AND MELINE WERE up before sunrise to handle things with Dante. The women drove in their new 2015 Lexus RC F Coupe that Dante had bought for them. Diamond called ahead to Fish Man to let him know that she was almost to Newark.

Diamond pulled up in front of the Hilton at which Fish Man told her to meet. She still had not told him about her friend, Meline. The women parked and then grabbed the bags that Dante had bought for them that were filled with new clothes and shoes.

"What type of car does he drive?" Meline asked as she and Diamond walked across the parking lot.

"Before he left Miami, he was driving a Range Rover," Diamond answered as she and Meline entered the hotel lobby.

Diamond walked through the lobby and headed to the front desk. She spoke with the desk clerk, only to find out there was already a room waiting for her.

She thanked the woman at the desk, checked in, and then took her key card. Diamond then led Meline to the elevator, and they rode up to the third floor.

"Are you gonna call him again?" Meline asked as the two found the room.

"I'ma call his ass once we get inside, girl!" Diamond answered as she opened the room door.

Just as she entered the room, the bathroom door opened up on her right side and Fish Man walked out.

"There goes my baby," Fish Man said, smiling as he grabbed Diamond around her small waist.

He was just about to pull her in for a kiss, but Diamond held up the bags she was holding and pressed them into his chest.

"Get my bags, Kyle!" Diamond told him, rolling her eyes as she turned back and took Meline's bags, which she also handed to Fish Man.

"Who's your friend?" Fish Man asked, staring Meline over hungrily with a devilish grin on his face.

Diamond noticed the look on Fish Man's face and how he was looking at Meline. She took Meline's hand and then pushed past Fish Man.

Diamond walked over to the bed, looked around, and said, "Couldn't you have gotten us a penthouse, Kyle?"

"It's good to see you too, Diamond!" Fish Man said, shaking his head as he walked over and set down their bags onto the bed.

He then turned to Meline, held out his hand, and said, "Allow me to introduce myself. My name is—!"

"I already know!" Meline told him, cutting him off. "My name is Meline."

Diamond cleared her throat loudly and interrupted the two of them: "I'm going to the bathroom to freshen up!"

She received no response from Fish Man, but she did catch Meline's eyes a moment. Diamond rolled her eyes as she walked off to the bathroom and then locked the door behind her. She dug out her phone from her Gucci purse and called the number to the bodyguard that Dante had assigned to her and Meline.

"Yeah!" Gage answered.

"We're in the room on the third floor. Room 103."

"I'm right outside your door now."

"Don't knock!" Diamond told him "Fish Man is in the room now."

"Are you and Meline okay?"

"Yes!"

"I'll get a room on this floor while you two are here. Call if you need me."

"Okay!" Diamond replied, hanging up the phone.

* * *

Dante dug out his phone from his pocket when he felt it vibrate. He was in the car on the way to the mall to spend some time shopping with his mother and sister.

He recognized Gage's phone number and answered, "Yeah?"

"Fish Man's with Diamond and Meline now! What you want me to do?"

"Relax!" Dante told him, understanding exactly what Gage was asking. "We're not gonna make a move yet. Once we've got what information we need, then lay 'im to rest!"

After a few more words with Gage, Dante hung up and slid his phone back into his pants pocket.

"I take it you've already made contact with this Fish Man person?" Brenda asked.

Dante looked over at his mother as she sat rolling the blunt she took from Tony T back at the hotel.

He then focused back on the road but answered, "He's at the hotel now with Diamond and Meline."

"Why don't you put a tail on him?" Brenda asked as she stuck the blunt between her lips and then held out her hand to Dante.

Dante handed his mother his gold lighter that Natalie had bought him as a gift, and grabbed his phone again to call Yasmine.

"Yes, my husband?" Yasmine answered on the second ring.

"Yasmine, I need a tail on Fish Man. He's at the hotel with Diamond and Meline now. Call Gage's phone and tell him to keep watch on Fish Man until the tail gets to the hotel."

Brenda smirked while she listened to her son take her advice.

She then handed Dante the blunt once he hung up the phone, and said, "If you're interested, I got a friend I want you to meet."

"We're not going shopping?" Dante asked, looking back at Melody through the rear-view mirror and seeing her on the phone.

"You can make it up to us later!" Brenda told him, but then held out her hand again and said, "Gimme your phone!"

* * *

Twenty minutes later, Dante was parked in front of a white and yellow house with a tall gate surrounding it. He sat watching a black E63 Mercedes-Benz slowly pull up alongside the new Audi A8 V10 Plus that Melody had talked him into buying. He reached for his Glock in his left holster only to stop when he heard his mother call his name.

"It's okay, sweetheart," Brenda told Dante. "This is the friend I spoke about. Let down your window."

Dante let down his window, just as his mother had asked. But he still pulled out his banger and laid it on his lap.

"Brenda Bell!" the male driver said from inside the Benz as he smiled across at her. "I haven't heard from you in some time now!"

"Hello, Patrick!" Brenda said, smiling at the driver of the Mercedes. "I want you to meet my son, Dante."

"Dante Blackwell!" Patrick said, finishing for Brenda after recognizing the driver of the Audi. "Who doesn't know the man who not only controls all of Miami but who's also defeated both the Miami Police Department and DEA!"

"Well, it's good that you know of my son, because there's a big favor I need to ask you to do for me, Patrick," Brenda began. "You will be paid $60,000 a month for your assistance."

"What am I assisting Mr. Blackwell with, Brenda?" Patrick asked her, even though he was certain what it was about.

"We both understand what's being asked here, Patrick! You either will agree or you won't! Decide!" Brenda told him, but this time no longer smiling.

Patrick stared across at Brenda, looked back over at who law enforcement called "the deadliest man in

America," and said, "Make it $80,000! I have to pay off a contact man for your son since he can't call me directly. My guy is gonna want $20,000!"

"Done!" Brenda replied. "You will have your first two payments by eight o'clock tonight!"

Brenda received a nod from Patrick before he put his window back up and drove off.

She then turned back and faced forward in her seat, and then said, "Let's go, Dante!"

"You gonna explain what just happened?" Dante asked, putting his window back up as he made a U-turn and drove in the opposite direction.

"Dante! Mama just introduced you to the chief of police for the NYPD," Melody told her brother as she sat forward in her seat and smiled at him.

"I'm not gonna ask how you know the chief of police, because I believe you would have told me if you wanted me to know!" Dante stated, but then he added, "You've been planning this since Melody called and told you that I was coming out here, haven't you?"

Brenda looked over at her son and said, "Before, Dante! I sent Melody to come and get you because there is something else I want you to do, and I will help you throughout it all! There's a lot that you and

I have to discuss to get you to understand who I am, Dante!"

Dante remained quiet for a few minutes and allowed everything to play out through his head.

He then asked, "Who's the person that crossed you, Mama?"

Brenda slowly smiled, looked over at her son, and said, "His name is Antonio Mitchell. He's the reason I first moved out here to Syracuse."

"Tell me about him!" Dante told his mother as he slowed the Audi and turned into a soul food restaurant he had spotted.

* * *

While the three of them found a table and ordered their food, they ignored the stares and pointing they received from customers who recognized Dante. Brenda then began telling her son about the story that Melody had already known about concerning Antonio Mitchell.

Dante listened to his mother open up and confess to cheating on his father, after finding out that he had gotten another woman pregnant not once but three times. Dante paid close attention when his mother told him about her weed connect that she had in Syracuse. She introduced Antonio Mitchell to the connect, who later got Brenda pregnant and then caused her to lose the baby after beating her up. He then left her for a white woman with whom he married and moved away.

After hearing enough of the story, Dante interrupted his mother, "Where's this dude at now, Mama?"

"Buffalo, New York!" Brenda answered. "I just got his address and even his cell and home phone numbers."

Dante nodded his head and then said, "I'll deal with it. You have any special request how you want the nigga to go out?"

"Just make sure he knows it's me who's ending his life, baby!" Brenda told her son as she reached over and gently rubbed the side of her son's extremely handsome face.

TWENTY

DANTE DROPPED OFF HIS mother and sister back home and agreed to bring Alinna and the rest of the family over for dinner later that night. Dante then drove back to the hotel and was just climbing out of the Audi when his phone began to ring. He dug his phone out of his pocket while he locked the car.

"What's up, Gage?" Dante answered, when he saw who was on the other end of the line.

"Boss! We may have a problem!"

"Problem?" Dante replied, walking into the hotel. "What type of problem?"

Dante listened to what Gage was telling him. He walked into the stairwell so the call wouldn't drop if he was on the elevator. After he hung up, he rode the elevator up to his penthouse and stepped off in deep thought. Dante made it over to his door and nodded to his security detail as one of the guards opened up the door to the suite.

Dante stepped inside the suite and saw Vanessa and Harmony sitting in the front room along with Alinna, Natalie, and Yasmine, who were eating sushi.

Dante barely made it fully into the front room when Alinna stood up and asked, "Dante, baby, what's happened? What's wrong?"

"Call the rest of the family here!" Dante said without answering Alinna's question.

He then turned and walked over to the sliding glass door that led out onto the terrace.

"Vanessa, get the others here!" Alinna told her as she then followed Dante outside.

She closed the door behind her, walked up to Dante, and asked, "Dante, what's going on? Something's happened, hasn't it? I can see it on your face!"

Dante told Alinna about the phone call from Gage and what he was told. He then pulled out his phone and handed it over to Alinna, and told her to look at the pictures that Gage had just sent him over a few minutes earlier.

Alinna stared at the pictures on Dante's phone and couldn't believe what she was seeing. But she instantly could see the problem that was to come from what she was staring at.

She looked back to Dante and asked, "So what are you going to do, Dante? You know what's going to happen once this is out and the family knows about this, right? How can we handle this?"

Dante remained quiet for a few moments just staring out over the city.

"I'll handle it! Just be on point, shorty!" he finally spoke up.

* * *

Once the family was all crowded inside the front room of his suite—minus Tony T, Dre, James, Kyree, and Gage, who were out handling business— Dante briefly explained to them about the problem they were facing. He then let everyone know that there was a traitor among the family.

"Who?" Vanessa asked, with her face balled up in anger.

"How do you know all this, fam?" Floyd asked as he and his team stood off to the side together.

"I'ma show you all proof, but if anyone reacts, I will deal with them myself!" Dante warned as he handed his phone over to Alinna.

She, in turn, handed the phone to Yasmine on her left and told her to look through the pictures.

While waiting for his phone to make its way back to him as each family member looked at the photos, Dante began to hear mumbling. He then heard the front door open, just as Dre and Tony T walked inside.

"What's going on in here?" Dre asked, looking around the room and seeing confused faces and pissed-off looks.

He noticed the cell phone being passed around and said, "What's going on, fam?"

"Come here, Andrew!" Vanessa told her man.

Harmony walked over to Tony T, grabbed his hand, and led him over to where she was sitting.

"What the fuck is this?" Maxine yelled, after looking at the pictures on the phone. "This is bullshit, Dante! These pictures don't mean a fucking thing!"

"Maxine, relax!" Alinna calmly told her.

"Fuck that shit, Alinna! These pictures don't mean shit!" Maxine yelled again.

"You feel that way?" Dante spoke up, drawing everyone in the room's attention onto him.

"Once he gets here, we'll see just how true these pictures are. And since you want to be the spokesperson, you'll also be the one to deal with this problem!"

"Dante, that's not right!" Keisha spoke up, standing beside her sister, just as the front door opened again and in walked James, Gage, and Kyree.

"What's going on up in here?" James asked, looking around at the expressions on everyone's faces.

"Gage!" Dante spoke up. "Close the door; and if anybody gets close to the door before we're done here, kill 'im!"

"Not a problem, boss!" Gage replied, closing the front door and then pulling out his banger and positioning himself in front of the now-locked door.

Dante turned his attention back to the family and saw that everyone was now staring at him. He pulled out one of his Glocks and noticed that James was now looking at the pictures on his phone.

"Maxine, come here!" Dante demanded.

Dante handed Maxine his banger when she walked over to him, and then he told James to let Kyree see the pictures.

"We now have everyone here. Now, let's see if what we've all seen is the truth or a lie! It's on you, Maxine! Handle your business, shorty!" Dante instructed.

To be continued . . .

"Text Good2Go at 31996 to receive new release updates via text message."

BOOKS BY GOOD2GO AUTHORS

GOOD 2 GO FILMS PRESENTS

THE HAND I WAS DEALT- FREE WEB SERIES
NOW AVAILABLE ON YOUTUBE!
YOUTUBE.COM/SILKWHITE212

SEASON TWO NOW AVAILABLE